DOROTHY EDWARDS

A
Strong and Willing
Girl

Illustrated by Robert Micklewright

A Magnet Book

First published in Great Britain 1980
by Methuen Children's Books Ltd
Magnet paperback edition first published 1982
by Methuen Children's Books Ltd
11 New Fetter Lane, London EC4P 4EE
Reprinted 1983
Text copyright © 1980 Dorothy Edwards
Illustrations copyright © 1980 Methuen Children's Books Ltd
Cover artwork © 1982 Methuen Children's Books Ltd
Printed and bound in Great Britain by
Cox & Wyman Ltd, Reading

ISBN 0 416 24590 0

For Helen Murdoch and her lovely wee Mum

CONTENTS

THE VICARAGE STEPS

When I look back on me young days, I don't ever remember a time when I wasn't working. I can't remember playing with five-stones or dollies or paddling in the river like me younger brothers and sisters did. I went to school off and on, though I don't remember much of that because I was so often kept home to help out. In fact, in the end I stayed home all the time because I was the oldest girl and me mam needed me.

Our two eldest boys (the ones that came after me) earned pennies stone-picking and rook-scaring on a farm. Sometimes they went out with a couple of coal shovels and an old pail, scraping up horse-manure from the roads to sell at backdoors for people to use on their gardens. They gave the money to Mam and she

9

put it away in a tin on top of the dresser until there was enough to buy them new boots.

I earned a bit myself, doing doorsteps, running errands and the like. We were living in a little low cottage near the big boatyard at Teddington then. Our dad was working at the yard – painting and varnishing the new boats – it wasn't his trade exactly, he was a house-painter, but the work was regular and he could get home each day for his midday snack. The cottage belonged to the owner of the boatyard. We moved to the other side of the town when Dad went back to his housepainting again.

There were six of us children when I first went out earning and another baby on the way as usual. In those days there was always a baby to come and one to be washed for. When I look back on them times, I always see me mam in her white cap that she always tied tight under her chin, and her patched apron with the bosom full of clothes-pegs, a baby on her shoulder and a couple of toddlers at her heels, stooping for parsley in the bed by the backdoor.

Me mam had been in high up service over at Ham before she married Dad and she kept her nice ways: always a clean cap and apron, and the wooden floors and table scrubbed till they were white and ridgy. Every morning the steel fender had to be rubbed with emery, and the kitchener blacketted with home-made polish before the fire was lit.

She couldn't abide dirt, couldn't our mam, so what she couldn't reach or stoop to, she gave over to me. She'd tell me the right way to do it, and stand over me to see I'd learned, so that by the time I was eight I could scour a board floor *and* make the sand-soap to do it with. I could scrub washing and leather windows and change babies, and because we were poor, I knew all the uses everything could be put to before it was worn out enough to be thrown away.

One day, I remember, I was outside in our back-yard, up on a box, pegging out the washing (I was small for me age even then) when the Vicar's wife called. Down the path she comes with her great petticoats sweeping dust, a basket on her arm full of cast-off baby clothes and a packet of tea.

Young 'Missus Vicar' (that's what we called her, though not to her face of course) used to be a Miss in the house in Ham where Mam had worked, so it made her very familiar. No 'Can I come in?' Just walked straight through the door without even a knock; we might have been doing anything! I used to think it was a liberty, but me mam was proud to have it so, for 'Missus Vicar' had been one of her charges when she'd been nursery maid at Ham, and she had a great affection for her.

When I'd finished the pegging out, I walked into our room and there she sat, with her dusty skirts all over my clean floor and young Lennie playing with the broken chairleg-on-a-string that he called Horsie, and Charlie and Edie patty-booing an old cotton-reel one to the other under the table, talking away to our mam as if there were only the two of them there. Poor Dad, who had hurt his foot on a rusty nail down the yard and was off work, sat scrooched up in a corner trying to keep out of the way. I went over and stood by him.

'Things must be very bad, Mary-Ann,' says Mrs Vicar, 'With your good man unable to work and so many mouths to feed?'

'It could be better, Miss – m'm'm I mean.'

So Mrs Vicar says what she'd come to say: would *I*

take on some regular odd jobs for pay. 'You've taught her well, Mary-Ann,' she says. 'She's a good little worker for her age. Of course I know she's a great help to you, but there are things she could do.'

She said she'd already spoken to one or two ladies who would like their kitchen fires laid or their doorsteps cleaned. She said, 'Ladies with only one maid often need a little extra assistance. And of course there

are the Vicarage steps – they have to be swept and whitened every day, even with two maids they present a problem. What do you think, Mary-Ann?'

No one asked what did *I* think, even though it meant I'd have to get up extra early every morning because the ladies' jobs would have to be done before eight o'clock. No one did ask what children thought in those days. Mam said it seemed a good idea, we did need the money. I didn't say anything, no more did Dad. Like me, he wasn't asked.

So there it was. I was out before it was light when, even though it was summertime, the air was still chilly with river mist, going off like one of the workmen on the way to the gasworks, or the scrubladies to the public houses. I quite liked that walk once I'd got over the shock of being wakened up so early.

One thing I didn't like much though was going by the Post-Office. The big doors at the side would be wide open and the postmen inside already shaking out the mail-sacks on to the big tables. The first time I went by one of the postmen let out a loud whistle behind me and made me jump out of me skin. I didn't half let him have it! It was a chap called Artie Lambert who lived near us. He'd only just got married and he ought to have known better than to lark about making people jump!

After that he was always looking out to cheek me and I'd give him tongue-pie for an answer. But I didn't really like it, even though it was only teasing – it used to make me feel little and lonely somehow. But the rest wasn't too bad. The work I mean, work never bothered me, though being a servant's servant is no joy. The way some of them maids bossed me, beggars on horseback ain't in it.

Mrs Vicar's cook was the worst. Nag, nag because I was filling the pail at the sink for me steps when she was wanting to fill the copper for Vicar's bath-tub. Nag, nag, nag for fears I'd slop the floor. Nagging all the time with a crafty word that showed she thought young Mrs Vicar favoured our family too much.

I liked doing doorsteps. First brushing off the dust and dirt, then washing them clean, and then chalking them all over with the grey hearthstone, and rubbing it soft and smooth with the wrung-out rag. I still like doing them. I reckon it's like magic the way that grey dries up so white! There was a long sweep of steps up to Vicar's front door, with a glass canopy over the top and a nook underneath them where the dust-cans stood. When every one of them steps had dried out they sparkled like the white cliffs of Dover on the picture postcards. I used to take our kids for walks past the Vicarage later in the day, just to see them steps.

Sometimes when I went out I'd get other things to do aside me regular jobs. One time at the Vicarage I stayed over because they'd got behind with the cleaning. That time the Vicarage was in a right old state of polish because young Mrs Vicar's godfather, who was a Bishop, was coming that afternoon to stay for a little holiday and the maids had got behind and the front hallway was still in a state.

I enjoyed doing that hallway – it looked so nice and 'churchified' when it was finished. There was a lantern with coloured glass that they'd taken down to clean that morning and the chain had broke, and the ma'ogany bannisters still had to be done and the mats took up and brushed – all before the family was about. *I* got the floor to wash (that was nice – all cream and white and black tiles – just like the church) and the 'brella stand: I had to tip out all the 'brellas and wash that big china crock inside and out (that was churchy too with lilies painted on it) and then open and shut the 'brellas by the back door to get the dust off. The things gentry want done!

I was just helping put the mats back, with the door open to help dry out a wet patch, when the postman come up the steps with some letters. It was that Artie Lambert again and when he sees me he grins and says, 'Ho, quite the little scrub-lady.' And I says, 'You mind your feet on me steps!' – because they were still damp-ish – and he puts out his tongue, the cheeky dog.

I got an extra tuppence for that work, so I was pleased and so was me mam. I wasn't pleased a few days later though. As soon as I got to the Vicarage Cook got on to me. 'Did you do them steps yesterday?' she says, all nasty. 'They were a disgrace if you did. All muddied up. And his Lordship here and all. You'll have to do better than that or I'll tell the missus.'

And that was a shame and a lie for I'd done those steps clean as clean. But I didn't argue. Only the next day it was the same. Dirt all up them steps again – first thing in the morning and I *knew* I'd done them proper!

I was upset when I got home and I told our Billy – he was next youngest to me – and Billy said it could be the penny-postman. He came round early. 'He must have overlooked the boot-scraper,' Billy says.

'But it's mud,' I tells him, 'and there's not been any rain for days. How'd he get mud on his boots? Less he does it a-purpose somehow.' I remembered the way that Artie Lambert had grinned at me when I'd said to mind me steps!

The more I thought the more wild I got. I've always had a temper. 'Fiery Nan' Dad used to call me.

'I'll *mud* him,' I says, 'I'll *mud* him. I'll make him *eat* it!' I kept on like this all day while I was helping Mam bring in the wash and warm up the irons. Mam told me I'd better not choke myself with spite 'till I was sure it *was* Artie. 'You just hold off till you've got proof,' me mam says. 'People can be took to court for defaming an innocent person.' And she took me to task for my nasty suspicions and Billy to task for giving me ideas.

So I tried to be fair, and by nightfall I was nice as pie and ready to think the mud could have grown on those steps.

· Next morning when I got up the mist was pinky with sunrise and I saw the long-legged birds pecking along the river edges where the water had dropped low from the tide. (Tide-ending-Town: that's what 'Teddington' means.) Most mornings the mud was showing below the banks. It made me think again of me steps, and I wondered if the birds could have brought the mud over and dropped it from their beaks.

I had just got to the Post-Office when who should come round the corner with a red wicker barrow full of letter-bags but Artie Lambert, whistling like a dicky-bird. When he sees me he gives that grin of his: 'Off to do the Vicar's steps, then?' he says. 'You mind you do them nice for that old Bishop,' he says, and he bangs his way into the Sorting Office, whistling and grinning. It *had* been him. I was sure of it.

I was so wild I felt me face go stiff and me fingers knotty (I always go that way when I'm really mad) so's I hardly know how I got to the Vicarage or anything. It was like 'swimming blind through a red sea!' like I once had read to me from a book somewhere.

Well, young I might be, but being eldest of a family I already knew how to stand up for myself. By the time

I'd done the Vicar's steps I'd thought up a plan to have my own back on that Artie.

Instead of going home when I'd finished, I filled me bucket again, and stood it underneath those front steps I'd just cleaned, and then I took up me place behind them near the dust-cans and waited for footsteps. I remember the smell of them stinky old bins to this day. It's a wonder I wasn't sick, but I stood the smell, until at last I heard what I'd been waiting for: footsteps coming up the street and stopping outside the Vicarage. I crept out with me bucket and looked up through the railings, and there they were – two boots, plastered with wet mud, on their way up my fresh steps. That

Artie! I'd give him grin!

I upped the bucket and swooshed upwards, getting some of the water back on me – not that I cared. 'That'll learn you!' I shouts. Artie lets out a sort of bleating noise and then he looks over the rail at me. And it wasn't Artie at all. It was an old gent in a black hat and a black coat, with a tiddler-net, and a water-jar on a string, full of swimming things that he came near to dropping on me.

It was the old Bishop, and wasn't he surprised? It seems he was spending his holiday netting little fishes and creatures from the river and looking at them through a peep-glass. He liked to get up early because some of the creatures bred in the wet mud. It seems that the birds poking about showed him where those creatures were hiding. (I heard later on he wrote little bits which got printed about those creatures he found.)

Oh, I did feel awful. Throwing water on a Bishop's boots and all! But the Bishop was very nice about it, and so was young Mrs Vicar, when I told her why I'd done it and about hiding by them smelly bins. She said Cook should have told me it was the Bishop who muddied the step, because she knew all about his going out early and that his boots were sent down on a newspaper to be cleaned directly after he'd changed into his slippers. I think she must have got on to Cook about it, as Cook was real bitter with me afterwards as if I'd been making deliberate mischief when I hadn't.

Still, I had been ready to think bad of that Artie Lambert and that I *was* sorry about. Next morning when I went by the Post-Office, I'd made up me mind to be nice to him if he was cheeky. But he wasn't, he was creeping round with a face like a wet week.

'Hello,' I says, 'You look fed up. Been putting letters

in the wrong doors?' After all, although he was married he wasn't all that old really.

'No,' he says, quite meek. 'But my missus is having the baby today and I can't help worrying.'

'Cheer up,' I says. 'People down our way are always having babies. Look at me mam. There's nothing to worry about.'

And I was right. When I got home that day Mam tells me Artie's missus had got a little boy.

'That means Artie's really grown-up now,' I says to Mam. 'No more larking about.'

'The beginning of his troubles,' says our dad, but he winks at Mam and she laughs.

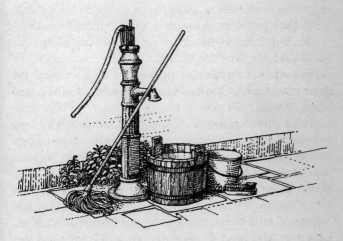

ALICE FROM THE ORPHANAGE
AND THE GOLDEN JUBILEE

I shall always remember the year 1887 for it was the
year of the Old Queen's Golden Jubilee – the year I
went out into service.

I was just past my tenth birthday by then. I'd done
jobs before that of course; minding babies and sweeping yards and cleaning doorsteps, but when I was ten
the Vicar's wife found me a place with two old ladies in
Richmond, a few miles down the river from us.

Of course, I cried when I left home. My mam and
my dad and the eight younger children cried too, but I
was the eldest and there wasn't room for me anymore
and Dad's wage went nowhere. I was the eldest, the
first to go, the others would follow when their times
came.

The house where I worked was one of those tall ones

on the Hill, just above the bend in the River – with black railings and square windows. Miss Gooch and Miss Hetty the ladies were called.

I remember my first day – them in their black dresses and mittens and lacy caps with purple bows, looking at me with their sharp eyes, and me in the new calico dress and coarse apron, with me hair all cropped and prickly under a plain cap.

'Do you know your Catechism?' asks one, and, 'Are you honest and truthful?' says the other, and, 'Yes-um,' I says, both times – for that's how you were taught to speak to ladies. 'Yes-um. No-um. Please-um.'

'Her parents are good, hardworking people,' says Miss Gooch to Miss Hetty. And then I broke down and cried a bit, so they tinkled a little bell and asked the other maid, a girl called Alice, to take me downstairs and show me me duties.

That Alice was a tall girl, thin as a spider with a grinning sort of cheerful face. Once we'd got on to the kitchen stairs she stopped and raised her eyebrows at me. 'Couple of old black crows, ain't they?' she says. 'Do this, do that, and mean as muck. But I works hard and they knows it – I work good enough for two. But then who wouldn't with all these fine things to see to?'

And she told me that she was fifteen years old and had been with the Missesses for the past three years. Before that she'd been in the Orphan Home. 'After all them bare boards and yellow blinds and tin plates this here is Heaven,' she tells me. 'I still like to rub me cheeks on the curtains and take a roll on the rugs when no one's about, because of the richness.'

But I began to sob again. 'We ain't got no rugs at home neither, but I'd rather be there,' I says. I did so want me mam.

'Cheer up little 'un,' that Alice says. 'After all, your mam's only a step down the river. I ain't never 'ad a mam as far as I know, and I ain't grizzling, am I?' And she gives me a hug and I makes a friend and things get a bit lighter.

The only other servant was old Mrs Corkett the cook. She was a poor old soul with bad legs who used to moan and groan all the time about the Missesses' meanness. 'Everything locked away and measured out each day like it was gold,' she'd say. 'How can I make anything tasty?'

She'd been used to working for rich people where there had been plenty of nibbling-bits and left-overs, but because she was afraid of the Workhouse she kept

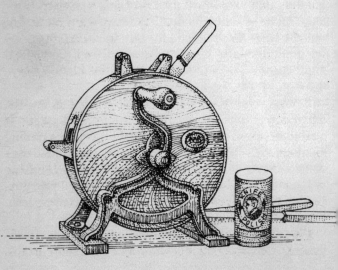

her complaining for downstairs and 'Yes-um'd' and 'No-um'd' to the ladies as much as I did.

But not that Alice! She spoke out quick as a flash if she thought she was being put upon. I used to wonder she wasn't sent off on the spot. But she was a splendid worker – quick as lightning. She actually enjoyed all the rubbings and the sandings, the carpet beatings and curtain washings that went on. I didn't, but she would sing away! And she'd answer the front door and serve drawing-room tea as grave as a butler. The ladies knew they'd got a treasure all right. So if she got a bit sharp they just frowned at her and told her to be more careful of her tongue. 'Those orphanage girls lack polish,' Miss Gooch would say.

Anyway, as I was saying: I started work in Richmond in the May of the Golden Jubilee Year and by the beginning of July everyone was going mad. 'Fifty Golden Years!' 'God bless Her Majesty!' Not quite so mad as they did when the Old Lady's sixtieth came up, but mad enough. Bonfires heaped up on all the greens and lanterns strung out between the trees in the gardens by the Thames, and red, white and blue flowers in circles planted in the Terrace gardens.

I forgot my homesickness as I trotted down the High Street with Alice and the shopping baskets. It was so exciting. I can remember the workmen nailing pictures of the Queen on to the wooden archways over the roadway, and the banners and bunting breaking out along the shop-fronts and the window-ledge gardens full of geraniums and petunias, and trailing fern. Oh, it was pretty!

One of the sights I remember was a big greengrocers, with swags of red, white and blue, like curtains

23

painted on the window-glass, and a great crown made of golden oranges and a pineapple sceptre in the centre. 'Orange for a golden crown,' says Alice. She was quite carried away.

It was lovely looking out from our attic window and seeing all the goings-on in the houses and meadows below. Banners and flags, and the maypole with its coloured ribbons, and the children practising, and the men touching up the boats with fresh paint:

As we made beds and emptied chamber-pots and sharpened knives and black-leaded grates, we chattered like two sparrows about the Jubilee Day. I can see that Alice now, with those long arms pegging out the sheets. 'It'll be nearly as good as seeing the Queen up London,' she says. 'The Mayor and his lady bowling down the street and the firemen and the military bands.'

And we plotted how we'd manage to slip down to the town and have a peep at the goings-on. Alice had her eye on a big old tree at the bottom of one of the gardens by the river. 'We could get in by the side alley past the bootmakers,' she tells me. 'We won't be noticed and we can take a good look from up there.'

Alice's excitement really got hold of me. Normally I was a pretty placid child but she did go on and on so. Lots of the houses around us were decorating their fronts with flags and streamers and flowers. 'Oh, I can't wait for us to do ours,' she says.

At last she couldn't bear it no more. 'Will you be putting the flags out soon, Miss?' she asks Miss Hetty when we were collecting the hearthstone and the brass cleaner for the morning. 'If you were, Miss, I could slip round next door and borrow their gardener's ladder before he puts it back in the barn.'

Miss Hetty went a bit pink. She was the softer one of the two Missesses. 'Well no,' she says. 'I don't think that will be necessary. Miss Gooch and I have been invited to stay in London to see the Celebrations. It's not as if we'll be in residence. It would be a waste of money to decorate the house when we're not At Home.'

That was a blow for us all right. No decorations! I thought Alice would burst into flames she was so mad. '*We'll* be at home, won't we?' she says the minute Miss had gone. 'Why shouldn't *we* have a bit of decoration?' I think she was wild because after all them grey times in the Orphanage she was itching for a chance to splash a bit of colour around, and I was because it made me feel cut off from the happenings down in the town.

'Mean old cats, grudging a bit of colour for the Old Queen, and us the highest house on the Hill,' Alice says. 'Everyone will notice and it will serve them right. Black – that's all they're interested in – like their stuffy old gowns!' And she clatters the crocks into the sink as if she meant to break them.

Mrs Corkett said she could see Alice's point, but at the same time she knew for a fact the Missesses hadn't always been like that. Mrs Corkett did a lot of gossiping with next-door's cook who had been there over thirty years and remembered when the Missesses' old father and mother were still alive. She hardly ever spoke to us about what she'd heard, in case something got back to the ladies, but seeing how wild Alice was she thought to calm her with a bit of gossip.

'They were quite a flighty pair when they were girls,' she says. 'Very lively.' And she told us that the Missesses had been packed off to the United States for a whole year to stay with Miss Hetty's godma who'd married a Yankee. The idea being that the hard life in America would bring them to their senses. But they came back giddier than ever, mad about American ideas and American fashions. 'Bright colours, and more like gentleman's fancy-dress,' was what Mrs Corkett had heard.

'Drove up in a carriage as bold as brass and their ma nearly dying of shock! The old gentleman had a bonfire made that very night and stood over them while they burned all that American finery. It caught some trees alight and the fire-brigade came out. It was a big scandal at the time,' she says.

'Anyway, the old gentleman took the Missesses in hand himself after that, very strict he was. By the time he passed on they're like we see them today.'

I don't think I quite understood all this at the time. It seemed a sinful waste to have burned good clothing, knowing how hard it was for our mam to dress us all decently. But Alice, thinking of all the bright coloured clothes going up in smoke gives a wail. 'Now they're like funeral mutes,' she says.

'Never mind, little 'un,' she says to me later when we were undressing for bed. 'It mightn't be too bad at that. Mrs Corkett ain't going to do any more minding of us than she has to. We'll be able to do as we like. We might even nip along to see your mam in Teddington. Mrs C. will never blow on us in case the Missesses were to give her notice!'

So we smirked and whispered and thought no end of ourselves with our plan for the Golden Jubilee. But then they were dashed for ever.

Mrs Corkett fell down the back kitchen step and hurt herself so bad she was took off to the Infirmary, which meant there'd only be Alice and me in the house over the Jubilee. Now what would the Missesses do?

Alice said they'd go all right, they wouldn't waste their new black silk shawls and bonnets. 'We won't half have larks then – we'll be able to stay out late for the bonfire and no one the wiser.'

'We can't disappoint our friends,' Miss Gooch tells us, very prim, 'yet we don't like the idea of you young girls roaming about on your own. We'll have to make arrangements,' and she goes off to talk to Miss Hetty.

'They're going to take us with them,' I says. 'We'll see the sights and the Queen in her carriage!'

'You've got some hopes!' Alice tells me.

We heard nothing more. The Missesses were taking the four o'clock train to Waterloo, and at three Miss Gooch went all round the house, closing and locking the downstairs shutters, bolting and barring the back-door, double-fastening the bedroom windows. Alice trotted behind with the key-basket. At last she couldn't bear it any longer. 'What are *we* going to do, Miss?' she asks.

'You'll be quite safe, no one can get in,' Miss says. She says she'd sent a note to the police station to ask the constables to keep an eye on the house.

'We are leaving food out for you, something good and simple you can prepare for yourselves and as a Jubilee treat, there'll be a tin of Abernethy biscuits and four slices of plum cake,' she says.

She says we needn't work tomorrow as it was a holiday and Miss Hetty says we'd get a good view of the maypole and the coloured boats from the attic windows.

You should have heard us after the key grutted in the front door lock and we heard the cab rattling off. I thought Alice had gone crazy. She ran through the house trying doors and windows, but it was no good – the place was as tight as a drum. She banged and shouted worse than one of my young brothers, and her a grown-up girl of fifteen! 'What about *our* Jubilee?'

'Not even a flag to wave,' I says.

Alice stopped in her tracks. 'Red, white and blue!' she says and snaps her fingers. 'You shall have your flag, for I've got an idea!'

She sent me down to the back scullery for the spare length of clothes-line and the strong pegs and told me to bring them up to our front attic. It was eerie going downstairs in the half-dark because of the shutters being up, and I was up in the attic in no time!

Alice was in the lumber room opening a trunk. 'I had a nose through this lot just after I first come here,' she says and starts throwing out a lot of old curtains. Then she took out a tray. 'Here they are!' she says.

'Take the clothes-line and peg them firm as I give them to you,' she says. There were some yellow cushion covers and blue shawls with fringes, purple aprons and big cotton handkerchiefs with flowers in the middle and red, green and pink borders. I pegged like mad.

'Leave the middle for the flag,' Alice tells me.

It was an enormous flag: red, white and blue all right – only stars and stripes instead a of criss-cross. Alice pegged it herself. On either side of it she fastened two big double bag things made of orange-coloured flannel. 'Gold for the Jubilee, like the greengrocer's,' she says.

When it was dark, Alice climbed out of our window and walked along the ledge behind the ironwork and fixed the ends of the rope to the hooks on each corner.

It took both of us to lower it over the edge, it was so heavy.

Then Alice went mad again. This time she danced and sang and jumped on and off the beds till she got me jumping too. Very, very late we lay with our heels on the bed-rails eating plum cake and laughing.

'They're lovely,' I says. 'And everyone will see them – everyone in the town I expect.'

'They will that,' says that Alice and she laughed and choked on her cake crumbs.

We were ages getting to sleep and next morning it was cheers that woke us up.

There were hundreds of people down in the meadows already to make sure of a good place. Among them were the Town Militia in their red uniforms. It was them who cheered. There was a great roar from everyone when we stuck out our heads to see what was up.

There was quite a wind that morning and our decorations were streaming out on the loose rope like washing; the cushion covers had filled out with it, and so had the orange bag-things. The flag was flapping madly.

'It's our decorations,' shouted Alice. 'They're cheering them!'

We saw everything from that window. The maypole, the mayor and the marching, the orphans in their grey cloaks and the carriages of the gentlefolk, and everyone looked up and saw us. It was like being queens.

All day long people streamed through the meadows. Some came right up the Hill and stood in front of our house. Some knocked on the door and one or two shouted through the letter-box but of course, we couldn't open the door, we were locked in.

Next day when the Missesses came back there was a terrible to-do. You see, they hadn't realised that their pa hadn't burned *all* the bits and pieces they'd brought from Yankee-land. The shawls and aprons, the stars and stripes flag and the bottom halves of their Bloomer costumes had been overlooked!

No one blamed me of course, I was only young, and no one had a chance to blame that Alice, for, as the ladies came in and made for the back-stairs, she slipped out into the street with her bundle under her arm and was gone.

She'd done it on purpose to upset the Missesses. You see Bloomers were thought to be very rude garments in them days and she wanted to show the ladies up. But as I said she had a crazy streak in her. I heard later she joined a circus. She'd have liked that – all the dressing up and the spangles!

THE BOYS WHO SHOULD HAVE
KNOWN BETTER

There was a lot of talk and indignance about what
happened over at Richmond: Alice and me being
locked in like that. Suppose there had been a fire or an
accident or something? It wasn't long before the
Vicar's wife heard about it. She went along at once to
tell our mam, full of guilt because she'd recommended
me there. She made such a to-do that Dad and our
Billy came over and fetched me back home.

After that, I just went out a-temporary for a bit,
coming home between whiles which suited Mam.
First I went to a place at Hampton Wick for a few
weeks to wait on the monthly nurse. Monthly nurses
were women who lived in a house when a lady was
going to have a baby, and stayed on for a few weeks
after. I wasn't there long before the baby came, and I

took over all its washing and the nurse's washing. After all the babies we had at home it was easy work for me.

I enjoyed that place, ironing the baby's things. Lovely long white robes and under-petticoats with lace on them, and flannel binders with blue stitching, and little round hats—because in spite of all the fancy lace it was a boy baby! And there was always lots to eat, and when the gentlemen friends of the family came, there was a shilling for me as a tip. I was very sorry when the permanent nurse moved in and it was time to go.

People who know me well have always called me headstrong. Well, I don't think I was always that way —more timid if anything – but a place I went to some time after that was the beginning of my head-strongness, I think.

I went to live in with an old lady who lived over the other side of the town. It was one of them tall, narrow houses on a slope, with the kitchens half underground, and a cellar below that.

This old lady was called Miss Ellum. She was a funny one all right. All ladies wore caps indoors in them days, but Miss Ellum had a bonnet on top of her cap as well. Most of the time she sat by the fire in the parlour, but sometimes she hobbled about the house on a stick. She looked very old and ancient I can tell you, all scrinkled up about the face and short-sighted with blue glasses. She sucked cloves all the time. I always think of her when I smell cloves.

As I said, the house was narrow, so the rooms weren't big. I had to sleep up the attic with the old servant who was called Anna, who was deaf as a post and muttered to herself. That attic was full of old Anna's bits and pieces, in bags and boxes under the bed and on top of the cupboard. Anna's dusty gowns and bonnets and boots were everywhere. There was candlegrease all over the bedside table and the matting underneath, and I don't reckon the window had ever been opened since she'd first moved in there. I had a little made-up bed over by the far wall where the ceiling sloped down. It was quite comfortable, and as I fell asleep every night as soon as I stretched myself out because I was so weary, I didn't mind Anna's untidiness after a bit, though what me mam would have said I can't think.

Them two poor old images, Anna and Miss Ellum had lived in that place for umpteen years – ever since Miss Ellum's father who had been a draper in Kingston had died and that was when Miss Ellum was still youngish. Anna had gone to scrub the place through before the furniture went in and had stayed there ever since, doing the housework, the shopping and all the mending. She was older than the old Miss, though you wouldn't have guessed it. I suppose that's because, like me, she'd always been a hard worker. It keeps you stringy and on your toes; ladies I notice tend to go to fat and floppiness when they're waited on hand and foot like Miss Ellum was.

It must have been hard on Anna when she began to find she couldn't manage no more – for there's one thing I'll say for that Anna right away, she really had kept things nice for her old dear. Messy her attic might be, and her not too clean about her person, but the part of the house that showed was still a credit to her.

But she had got slow. She had trouble lifting and bending and she moved like a snail, and when I bellowed in her ear to ask what I was to do next she had to

get her wits together to tell me. And that was when I started getting headstrong. I got tired of waiting for me orders (after all, they'd wanted a strong and willing young girl, and that was me), so I just looked around and saw what wanted doing and went at it without asking.

I might be a Little Titch but I'm all there, quick and strong. If I was to show you me arm and leg muscles even now, you'd whistle. In them days I hadn't got me muscles fixed but I was starting to grow them!

And that old Anna was pleased. She muttered away so nicely to herself about me it went to me head. I lifted furniture and unhooked curtains and cleaned lamps and beat carpets and really enjoyed meself having me own way. Once I got going that old Anna was like putty in me hands – she doing less and less and me more and more. She kept muttering, 'That good gel, that handsome young worker,' to herself, and she dished me lovely dinners, stews and pies, same as old Miss and generally petted me.

Do you know, I got quite fond of them two old ducks and living in that narrow house. Once I'd got it to rights it was easy for us to keep things going, for old Miss didn't have many callers. When the old dear was abed we'd sit down in the kitchen with two lit candles on the mantelpiece, and our toes on the fender and make toast in front of the range. It was lovely, with beef dripping and a pinch of salt on it. We didn't talk much because of old Anna's being deaf, but it was quiet and friendly, quite a change from me home. I reckon it must have been pretty lonely for Anna before I came.

And then suddenly, trouble started. It came quite sudden one evening when the days was drawing in.

Anna was upstairs helping Miss to bed when there came a loud ring-ring from the front door. There was a row of bells in the kitchen and the front-door bell was an extra large one and stood at the end. I never liked that bell. When it stopped ringing it went on jerking and quivering for a bit in a very creepy way. That evening it didn't stop, it just jangled and jangled.

I knew Anna couldn't hear, so I took down a candle and set off up the kitchen steps and across the hall to the front door. I took a time with the bolts because I had to get a chair for the top one, and I'd just begun to turn the knob when the jangling stopped and someone shouted, and I heard feet running like mad down the road, and boys laughing and shouting. I ran to the front gate and was just in time to see some lads shooting round the corner.

After that it happened night after night. Sometimes they pushed open the letter-box and shouted things like 'old witches', sometimes they just rang the bell and ran away at once.

Anna never heard them but old Miss did. She used to get frightened and call out to know what was going on. It's not nice being old and helpless upstairs when anything might be happening down below.

When Billy and me was little there used to be an old girl at the top of Watts Lane as was so dirty you might have thought she had been black-leaded. She was balmy, poor soul and used to keep peeping and pointing out of her window. We would pretend she was an old witch, and thumb our noses at her and run away, till our mam found out and gave us a good talking-to. I think that's what those boys were up to.

Poor old Anna *did* look a bit freakish in her old-fashioned clothes, all bent and bony and muttering to herself as she went to the shops. She was a bit eerie. And old Miss sitting up at her bedroom window a-mornings while Anna cleared the slops must have looked a rare old Granny Bendybones with her bonnet on her cap and her blue eye-glasses. Them boys was just playing a game without thinking they might be hurting someone's feelings, just like me and Billy had done.

But at that time I didn't see it that way. I was just wild with rage. The sauce of it! So, being headstrong by now, I made a plan. I didn't tell Anna nor no one. I decided to set a trap.

It was one cold and foggyish night and there was a big laurel bush aside the front door. When Anna was up helping old Miss to bed, I opened the cellar door that was under the kitchen stairs. Then I went up to the hall and let myself out of the front door, fixing the latch so it wouldn't click shut and drawing it to. I'd blown out the candle so there was no light coming through the glass, and it was pitch-dark as I slipped behind the laurel bush and waited.

The boys came quite soon. Three of them there was. At once they began pulling away at the bell handle, jangle-jangling it and laughing. Then one of them bent to see through the letter-box and of course, the door went inwards taking him off balance and that was my chance. I jumped out with a great yell. My popping out like that startled the other two so much they just took to their heels.

In the meantime, I'd grabbled the one inside and with him kicking and shouting all the way (I told you I was strong) I ran him through the darkness down the hall, down the kitchen stairs, and pushed him into the cellar and slammed and bolted the door. Then I nipped back up again and shot the front-door bolts.

You should have heard the noise that boy made. Banging and kicking the cellar door and shouting, but I was still so mad, I thought, 'You just bang, mate.'

The other boys came back and rattled the letter-box and called out very soft, 'Are you there, Fred?' and I crept up to the door and shouted back, 'He's here, and he's going to stay.' Shouting sudden like that I must have made them jump. Anyway, I scared them, I heard them run off again.

By now Anna was down. She saw the cellar door shaking but she could only hear very faintly. Upstairs old Miss Ellum was calling out and thumping with her stick. I made Anna sit down in the kitchen and then I went upstairs to old Miss to tell her what I'd done. I'd thought she would have been pleased with me, but instead she was frightened out of her wits. She sits up against her big bolster with her eyes without the glasses all blinking under her nightcap starting to run with tears.

'Oh dear,' she says, 'what'll we do if that brute gets out? He will murder us all!'

Then it was my turn to be scared. I just hadn't thought about that boy Fred getting himself out of the cellar. Come to think of it, I didn't really know how big he was. I'd grabbed him in the dark, you see. He had given me some awful kicks that up to then I hadn't given much thought to. I went downstairs and rolled down me stockings and saw there were some great big black bruises on me legs, and, listening to the crashing and thumping on that cellar door I began to wish I hadn't been so rash. As for poor old Anna – she still didn't know what to make of it all – she sat looking at me in surprise with her poor old mouth all open.

I had just made up me mind to arm meself with the kitchen poker and try to murder the villain before he murdered us, when there come another ring at the front door. Not a long jangling one this time, but a short sharp one. It stopped for a bit and then started again, short and sharp. Not like the boys at all. Of course, they might have been trying a trick, but I had to risk that, so I nodded to Anna and made my way up to the front door again. This time I didn't try to unbolt it, I shouted, 'What do you want?' through the letter-box.

I can't tell you how glad I was when a man's voice said, 'Police, will you open the door, please?' A Bobby! I was so glad I began to cry, and I nearly fell off the chair I was so hasty to get them bolts back.

It was a Bobby all right. A great big policeman with a bull's eye lantern that he flashed round the hall. Then he opened his eyes very wide:

'Is the lady in, missy?' he asks me.

'That's old Miss upstairs,' I says, and I couldn't help it, I started to really sob. 'That's her rapping her stick. She's wondering what's happening.'

'These two boys here,' the Bobby says, 'they ran into me down the road and nearly dragged me here with a tale someone had got a friend of theirs inside against his will, reckons it was a great strong old woman as did it.' And then I made out two boys standing just ahind him.

'No it wasn't,' I says, crying and crying by now – daft, I couldn't stop, 'It wasn't no strong old woman neither, it was me.'

And, 'Oh sir,' I says, 'Please go and let him out. I locked him in the cellar and old Miss is afraid he'll break out and murder us, and Anna doesn't know what's up, and I can't bellow in her ear and tell her 'cos he's making such a row.'

'Is that him?' the Bobby says, for that boy was thumping away, and I says, 'Yes sir,' still snivelling and snuffling like a baby.

'Well, we'd better let him out then,' says the Bobby, and down to the kitchen we goes. The policeman pulled back the bolts on the cellar door and that boy came out.

Poor old Anna had comed up from her chair and stood staring like mad trying to make out what was happening: first at the Bobby and now at the boy. I stared too. I stopped crying and stared.

That boy had been crying too. His face was all black with coal-dust and streaky from tears. He didn't look a bit fierce, just frightened. And something else – he was a tidy bit bigger than me – a good head and shoulders I'd reckon. He wasn't half glad to see the Bobby.

But he wasn't so glad when the Bobby started asking him questions, because the more he told his story the fiercer the Bobby looked.

'Ringing bells and shouting through letter-boxes and frightening innocent old parties is a serious thing,' he tells this Fred. 'You could have been sent away for doing something like that, but I reckon you've been punished enough.'

He said if we didn't want to charge that Fred, he'd let him off this time, and I said I didn't so long as he promised not to upset us again. Anna didn't say anything because she couldn't hear what we were talking about, but the Bobby seemed to think my word was enough, so he made Fred say he was sorry and he took him upstairs and out of the front door to join the other boys.

It seems that Bobby went home with each boy in turn, and spoke to their fathers, and from what I heard afterwards, each father gave his son a good hiding – as fathers used to in them days.

A nice thing happened afterwards though. Next Saturday and for many Saturdays after, them boys came round in the morning to help weed the garden and run errands for us. I think in the beginning it was the Bobby's idea. Afterwards they came anyway, and we got quite fond of them. When a few months afterwards poor old Miss Ellum died, they were as sorry as I was that the house would go to someone else and there'd be no need for them to come round anymore.

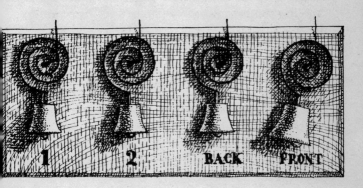

MR BUTTON'S SECRET

Some of the places I had when I was young weren't *that*
genteel. Just helping out ordinary people like the time
I went to Mr Button.

Mr Button was Head Coachman when our mam
first went in service at Ham. At that time he and Mrs
Button lived over the stables. Mrs Button had been
cook at the House and even after she was married she
used to oblige when there was a big party on. Mam
told us that Mrs Button had a special way of working
pastry up fancy that no other cook had; she had even
been praised by the Duchess of Teck, who was old
Queen Mary's mother and lived nearby.

When me mam first went to live in she was very lost
and lonely and Mr and Mrs Button were good to her;
she said she could always go over to the stables for a

laugh or a cry or a bit of cake. After she left service to marry our dad she still kept in touch with them. They had a girl of their own called Lily, who was a widow-woman that had been married to someone over Kew way who'd had to do with the Gardens. She'd done well for herself and had her own servant and was too stuck up to have much to do with them, so in a way I suppose Mam filled her place in their lives.

When the old Sir died he left a house with a bit of land and a nice sum of money to Mr Button, so they gave up service and settled down and raised chickens and grew vegetables and went out for airings in a little blue trap pulled by an old pony called Jackie.

It was a nice house, too big for two old people, with four bedrooms and two parlours and a big kitchen. It seems Mr Button and the old Sir had been boyhood friends, larking about together fishing and boating and the like, and the Sir had always had a tender spot for him. Sometimes, of a Sunday, mam and dad would walk us over the river bridge and across Ham Fields to take tea with the Buttons, and Mr Button would tell our Billy about the good times he used to have when the Sir was a lad. (Billy was Mr Button's special favourite.)

When the Buttons were set up so respectable their daughter Lily took to visiting them too. As she'd never had any children us lot were more than welcome, for Mrs Button doted on children – she was like another granny to us.

Then all of a sudden Mrs Button died. One warm day – there she was standing by her back door shucking peas into a bowl – all of a sudden she fell down dead leaving the poor old man to fend for himself, which must have been very hard for him because she'd always looked after him very well.

'She must have thought it would happen,' Mr Button told me mam. 'I found she'd left me a little letter in the dresser drawer, telling me what to do if she was ever took sudden like her own mother had been. She always thought ahead for me,' he said.

Mam made us all black arm bands and we went over for the funeral. That was the first time I ever saw that Lily: Mrs Watts she was, and what I saw I didn't take to. She was all in black, with a nose like a beak and a big white handkerchief with a black border and two beady eyes without a tear in them. For another thing, she took no notice of the other mourners – the nice old folk mostly pensioned off and married servants from the old days – not even a nod, and she certainly didn't fancy our family as a crowd, though, after the old lady was buried she came over and beckoned our mam over for a bit of a talk.

That's how it was arranged that I should walk over every day and clean and cook for the old man and take back his bits of washing for our mam to see to.

'That one's well above herself,' me mam said afterwards. 'If it wasn't for the dear old chap I'd tell her to look down her nose at someone else. But at least he knows us.'

When I first went to help Mr Button there wasn't a lot to do in the house. They'd only furnished a couple of rooms with the stuff they'd had over the stables. Mostly I helped him in the garden – weeding and suchlike.

It wasn't long though before the work started piling up on me. That Mrs Lily Watts began to come over too often. You could see what she was up to straight away – she was bent on making her father genteel.

I'd only been there a couple of weeks when she turns up with a uniform dress for me to clean and alter for meself, because she said I had to remember me place as I was being paid for me services (sixpence a week, I think it was). What an outfit that uniform was! Three times too big for me: a greasy old black gown that smelled of coughdrops and a set of old, yellowish aprons. 'They must have come out of the Parish Rag Bag,' me mam says. But we got down to them and the next time that Lily paid a visit I was wearing a clean black gown that fitted me, and a bleached and starched apron. (Mind you, I had some nice print dresses and good caps and aprons of me own from Miss Ellum's time, but Mam said not to mention that. After all, I'd be needing them later on when I could be spared to live in full time again.)

It's funny, looking back, for old Mr Button never said a word about me servant's get-up. In fact, for a long time he was so downcast he didn't seem to notice anything. He didn't seem to mind when all of a sudden Mrs Watts turned up with a covered cart and her own bed and bits and set herself up in one of the spare rooms to help her father settle, as she said.

But if he didn't mind, I did. No weeding the garden for me after that. Rub and scrub and shake mats and dust. All the rooms were opened up. And it didn't stop there either. 'We'd better get a man along to look at the tiles before the winter comes.' Then it was: 'We'll have the painters in and the paperers and get the place done throughout.' And the poor old man would hand over the money as meek as a mouse.

I did notice one thing though. Mr Button was getting more thoughtful than downcast, and now and again, when the cleanings and paintings were at their

height, he'd harness up old Jackie and climb up into
the little trap and off he'd go.

I can't say I blamed Mr Button. The place was
really uncomfortable. I only wish he'd asked me to go
with him, I'd have been glad to take turn-about driving Jackie. It began to look as if Mrs Watts wasn't
going to be in any hurry to go home either. I think Mr
Button must have begun to wonder a bit because he
kept giving her straight looks.

Then one day she let the cat out of the bag. She told
him that she had let her Kew place furnished to a
foreign gentleman who was doing something special at
the Botanical Gardens for a few weeks. Her servant

woman was looking after this gentleman and his wife, and no doubt, knowing that Lily, she was also keeping a sharp eye on the towels and cutlery. For the way she 'spicioned me was chronic – I caught her many a time peeping into my little apron bag and feeling my jacket pockets. Once, she put my jacket back so quick because she heard me coming, it missed the hook and fell to the kitchen floor, but she looked at me brazen and never said a word.

Mrs Watts let it out casual, but I got a nasty feeling there might be more to it than that. She might begin to make a habit of lettings! I was peeping through the crack of the kitchen door and I could see Mr Button's face, and I began to wonder if he was thinking that too!

Anyway, he just went off in the trap and we didn't see him again till it was nearly time for me to go home, and after that he took to driving off every day. Poor old man, I couldn't blame him, though I must say I began to wonder what he did with himself.

It was our Billy who opened my eyes. He came to meet me one evening. Billy and I were always very close and he knew I'd been worrying about the old chap. 'Old Mr Button,' he says. 'I've seen quite a bit of him over our way lately.' (Billy had taken a job in the tanyard at Kingston – it didn't last long though, because he hated the stink.)

'At least,' Billy says, 'Not him so much, but Jackie and the trap. He leaves it standing outside.'

'What do you mean, *outside*?' I says, and he says, 'Outside *The Boatman*'s – you know, that little public down by the water. He spends a lot of time in there,'

Billy says. 'But don't let on to his Lily, or she'll skin him.'

'She's drove him to drink!' I says.

Before I'd gone out to service I used to belong to the Band of Hope down at the Temperance Hall and I'd listened to people talking about how they'd been saved from strong drink, and looked at the magic lantern show of pictures of drunkards seeing green rats and what their insides looked like from taking too much. It used to give me terrible nightmares. In fact, if it hadn't been for the buns and cocoa they gave us, I don't think I could have borne it. My, that cocoa was lovely! All thick and dark and sugary – they didn't ruin it with milk like they does nowadays.

I wasn't half upset! But Billy says, 'I didn't say he was *drinking* at *The Boatman*. Just a drop warmed up to keep the cold out and a bit to eat I reckon, and a bit of comfort too, I shouldn't wonder. You couldn't blame him with that harpy unsettling the place the way you say she does.'

'But Mr Button at a public!' I says, for we thought publics were very common in them days.

'It's a nice little place,' says Billy, 'And run very strict so the men at the tan-yard say. And I'll tell you something that'll surprise you: Mrs Button used to go there with him sometimes!'

'Billy! You're making it all up,' I tells him. And he wouldn't say another thing. Just grinned at me. Our Billy was a great aggervater. I believed what he said about Mr Button, but the rest of it was too far-fetched. I could never believe that old Mrs Button would have done anything *low*.

I did wish Mr Button would face up to that Lily though. It began to look as if she wouldn't be satisfied until she'd spent all the Sir's money. What do you think she got on to him about next? Furniture! A parlour-set with buttoned backs, curtains, carpets and fire-irons: plush overmantels and everything.

And he gave in. 'You're probably right, Lily,' he says, 'I suppose this place don't strike comfortable to someone who's used to a more stylish way of living.'

'Poor old man,' me mam says, 'What does he want with that sort of thing at his time of life? Oh, she's feathering her nest all right, for from what I've heard her place over Kew isn't *that* grand. She'll sell it, you see!'

'I'm glad I'm temp'ry,' I said, 'because I couldn't stay there with her in charge. There's too much "Girl-this" and "Girl-that" for me.'

I must say though that when the new furnishings came and I helped to hang them plush curtains with the bobbles on I couldn't help thinking how lovely it all was.

Then it was time for Mrs Watts' lodgers to go back to their foreign land, and she had to go off to see to things. 'You can manage for a few weeks,' she says to old Mr Button, and off she went.

'A few weeks,' says Mr Button to me. 'We'll have to crack a whip before they're over.' I didn't know about him, but I reckoned I would, with all the tasks I'd been left with.

I thought Mr Button might stay at home now, but he didn't – he went off as before. I didn't mind much because the next couple of days I was very busy washing out the new linen and hanging it to bleach in the sunshine. It was so warm I remember that though it meant quite a trot from the fire-grate with them hot irons, I set a table up outside the kitchen door where I

could iron in the shade.

I'd just finished damping down the last of the bolster-cases when I heard the trap drive up. Mr Button was early! I went indoors and shifted the kettle from the back of the hob so it'd boil quickly. I knew he'd like a cup of tea.

Then I heard voices: one of them was our Billy's! I ran out and there he was – our Billy grinning all over his chops with a rose in his cap, and there was Mr Button with a rose in his coat, and hanging on Mr Button's arm was a nice fat old lady in a smart brown gown and a white shawl and bonnet with a bunch of roses in her hand.

'This is the new Mrs B.,' the old man says. 'We got hitched up this morning. Young Billy here was our best man.'

'Billy!' I couldn't believe he'd have been so artful.

The new Mrs Button was ever so nice. Really jolly and lively and such a bustler. In no time she had her bonnet and shawl off and was helping me lay the tea. We all had it together sitting round the parlour table.

'I can see Mr Button won't need my help any more,' I said to Billy, as we walked home over the Fields. 'She'll be able to manage all right.'

'She ought to be able to,' he said, 'She's looked after *The Boatman* single-handed since her husband died.'

Billy-know-all also told me that the new Mrs Button had been the first Mrs B's best friend ever since they were girls. In the letter she'd left she'd told Mr Button she'd like them to marry. Mr Button wouldn't have thought any more about it if Lily hadn't shown such signs of wanting to move in for good.

Even then, if Lily hadn't started on the house, with the painting and furniture and everything he'd never have had the courage to ask her to give up such a cosy and well-furnished home as she'd made for herself at the public.

Once she'd said, 'Yes', he thought they'd better get married quickly before Lily tried to interfere. 'He can't stand her, even though she *is* his daughter,' Billy said.

'I wonder what she'll say?' I said to Billy.

'She didn't say a thing,' he told me. 'Yesterday I took over a letter asking her to come to the wedding – the new Mrs B. thought it was only right.'

'She didn't say anything?'

'No,' says Billy. 'She slammed the door in my face. So close it nearly took me nose off.'

He didn't half laugh then. 'She slammed it so hard, a notice that was stuck in the side window fell down. I saw it go. It had FOR SALE written on it!'

Our Billy could certainly keep secrets while it suited him!

PHOTOGRAPHS

Until our Edie was old enough to be a real help to Mam it looked as if it would be better for me to go out temporary so's I could be back home when it was time for a new baby. I filled in at quite a few places before I went to my Miss Johnson's at Twickenham. I was fifteen by then and I stayed with the old dear for twenty-six years, right up until she died in fact.

I must have been about thirteen when I went to live in at a place the other side of the town; near to Bushey Park it was. A woman our mam knew called Mrs Atts got me this place. She went there as a morning scrub-woman. The servant they were taking on regular had to work out a quarter's notice, so I'd be needed about three months.

Mrs Atts said, 'Don't worry – you wouldn't be

overworked; they ain't particular so long as things get done somehow.'

Mam said afterwards that no one who could have put up with that dirty Fanny Atts for so long would be particular, but she said that didn't mean I was to be slack if I was took on. I'd best remember I'd got a fussy mam who'd trained me proper and not go slummocky whatever the temptation, or she'd have something to say to me!

I got the surprise of my life when I saw who me new Master and Missus were to be, for I recognised them at once. They were often down our part of the town; him

with a big straw hat on and a curly pipe in his mouth and her with a red shawl and old-fashioned bonnet, walking floppy because, as Mam said, she never wore *stays*. Dad always said they dressed funny because they were artistical: 'Boheemymums' he called them.

Anyway, in I walked and there they were: him in a cordurory coat and red neckercher like a road work-man and her with her hair frizzed up in front and netted behind, lolling on chairs with their feet on a big footstool: Mr and Mrs Philo Portman, if you please! They never asked for references or nothing. The lady just said, 'Good, you've come then. When can you start?' and that was that.

Mr Philo Portman had one of them photograph machines on legs, and when he found a place along the river bank he fancied, he stood about taking pictures of boats and swans and lock-keepers and things while Missus Philo Portman sat on her shawl making tea in a little shiny kettle over a spirit flame. When we were little we used to stand and stare at them for ages but they never seemed to mind.

Some of the young 'uns down our way used to reckon that Mr P. P. was wrong in the head, and they'd stand along the tow-path watching his antics, all ready to run like mad if he ever really broke out, but he never did. He would stand staring at the thing he wanted to make a picture of, and then go off and stare at it from somewhere else, then he'd look at it through a square picture-frame on a stick thing, then he'd push his head under a black curtain behind his camera, and then out he'd pop again! It certainly looked mad!

Mr P. P. had wanted to take a picture of us once, but he kept us hanging about so long that our Lennie, who was the baby at the time, started to cry for his dinner and we had to move off before he was ready to start his machine. Our mam was sorry when we told her because she thought he might have given us the picture when he'd done with it. It would have been nice to look back on. As it is, there aren't any childhood pictures of us older ones in the family collection so we shall never know what we used to look like in them days. When I went into service with the Philo Portmanses, Mam kept hoping Mr P. P. would fancy a picture of some of us and kept hinting at me to ask him, but I never liked to.

Mrs Atts told me that the Master's photographs were well thought of in artistic places. He used to paint and draw pictures till he took up the photographing. She said some of his pictures were used in books with bits of poetry under them.

'Down *The King's Head* there's a picture of Teddington Lock and some swans, with poetry under it, that the landlady cut out of a lady's paper and had framed. It's got "P. Portman" under the picture bit,' Mrs Atts said.

The Philo Portmans had a nice-looking little house with yellow roses all over its front and a biggish garden behind. The front was very pretty but the garden looked rubbishy to me. There was a fountain with stone steps going up to it, and a bit of old wall with a window in it and nothing behind, and lots of stone pots and statues. Mrs Atts told me Master used them in his pictures. She said sometimes people came and dressed up and were made into pictures for picture postcards. 'You certainly see things in service,' Mam said when I told her.

There wasn't a lot for me to do at the P. P'ses. There wasn't much in the way of carpets and rugs. Inside was very bare with white curtains and jars full of feathers and old poppy heads, and hard old black chairs and straw mats, which Mrs Atts said was supposed to be artistical, though I thought it looked poverty-struck.

There was something though that really did please me. In the back garden there was a sort of white summer-house that had green slat-blinds to the windows all round it so you could bring them down whichever side the sun was too powerful. When I started there there were apples and pears on all the wall-trees round the garden but the weather was still warm enough to need those blinds of an afternoon. So one of my jobs was to keep them moved because of the summer-house carpet. That was a job that did take my fancy – it was so *skilled*: you pushed in a china knob to send them up and you pulled it out to bring them down. They were the only blinds I ever saw worked that way; up with a snap and down with a click! I could have played with them for hours.

Because there wasn't a lot of real hard work for me to do, and the Missus didn't seem to mind, I used to dish up the tea and then pop off home for an hour to see me mam and the others and then be back in time to do the supper. In the evenings I'd sit with me workbasket patching sheets or hemming round the Master's old shirt-tails for dish-dryers for something to do, for no one ever told me to. (Them P. P'ses were the only better-off folk I ever came by who didn't use nice, properly hemmed wiping-up towels with 'nitials on. Till I went there they just used any old worn-out clouts they happened to have by them like the poorest people did. Mam used old rags and bits but she always hemmed them respectable.)

I didn't seem to have any special jobs given out, but

as I was already used to service I just did the things Mrs Atts hadn't touched and saw to the food. There were mostly two kinds of people who came to the house, the P. P'ses' friends like the people who had their pictures took for picture postcards and the folk who wanted to be took for their family albums. The friends and such used to come in at the side gate without being asked, but the others used to knock at the front door and be shown into the front parlour by me. I was always polite to the album customers, and sometimes they gave me a penny.

Some evenings our Billy would come through the side gate for a warm and a talk while I got the supper together. When we'd been little we'd often talked about the blow-outs we'd have if we were ever well-off, and he used to laugh when he saw what my Master and Missus ate. 'More like a navvy's dinner,' he used to say. 'Them big loaves and lumps of cheese and bowls of onion broth.' Oh well, they weren't like ordinary better-off people that's for sure. I suppose 'boheemy-mums' eat that way.

Now, our younger brothers and sisters always liked to hear about the goings-on at all the places I worked in, but it was the Philo Portmanses one that really took their fancies; in fact, they got so curious they took to hanging about near the house. Every time I leaned out of a window to give a duster a shaking I seemed to spy one or two of Ours peering over the gate. I had to speak to me mam about it in the end.

'It's them blinds,' Mam says. 'They are always on about them.'

'Well, they won't see them from the gate,' I tells her. 'And anyway, I wish they'd keep off. Missus hasn't minded Billy but she might carry on if the rest were trooping in and out.'

But I'm soft. One day (coming up to February it was) with the roads snowy the Master and Missus arranged to go off to London for the day. So I thought, Mrs Atts being laid up with a cold, why not have one or two of the littlest ones in to see the blinds. The youngest twins and Freddy had had the fever that winter and still looked a bit low spirited.

So I had a word with Billy: 'Wrap them up well,' I said. 'It's chilly outside even when the sun's on the garden.'

Next morning the P. P'ses went off, and an hour or so later, our Billy arrives with little Tottie and Phillie and Freddy, with big shawls pinned round them and clean old sacks on top for extra warmth, dancing with excitement.

I'd got the summer-house open and though it was cold the sun was streaming in one side. The shutters were closed, but it it didn't take a jiffy for me to nip round pushing the buttons, while the young ones stood beaming. My goodness you'd hardly credit how much pleasure they got from them. When I'd been alone in the house before, I'd made up a lovely game with them blinds, running round the room, clicking them up or down without stopping – push a knob in, pull a knob out, with some up and some down, and then changing over. It was a bit like the maypole dancing the children do at school, all chopping and changing. I played that game now and soon those kids were in fits! 'Let me try, let me try,' they shouted, and there we all were, snapping and clicking blinds up and down like mad, yelling with excitement and making such a din of it that we didn't hear the Master until he'd actually climbed the step and walked into the summer-house.

He'd only seen the Missus on to the train and then walked over to Hampton Wick to do some shopping. My word did he sound off! What on earth were we doing? Who were these children, etc., etc.

He looked so wild the young ones started to cry. One minute they'd been rushing about, all happy and rosy, and now, in a minute they'd dropped into little pale, fevery ghosts.

Our Billy didn't cry though. He went white and stiff and said, 'Please sir, 'taint my sister's fault. They just got on and on at her to show them those blinds, and how they clicked up and down, and because they'd been poorly she gave in to them.'

Mr Philo Portman stopped carrying on then. He looked hard at our little 'uns. He started to walk round and peer at them.

'Look,' he says, 'you've given me an idea. How would you like to earn yourself a penny each? How would you like to be in a picture?'

They didn't understand what he meant, but Billy did, he said, 'What do you want us to do, sir?' The Master said, 'Not you, lad. You're too robust. It's the young ones.'

I remembered how me mam had asked me to get round the Master for a picture of at least some of us, so I says quick, 'Would Mam be able to see it?' And he said, 'Oh, yes. I will send her a print.'

Then he told me to go and make some cocoa for all of us, while he took the picture. So I did. It was the first time the little ones had ever tasted cocoa and they ran their fingers round and round the mugs afterwards to get the sugar off the bottoms.

Billy told me the Master had put the little ones to stand by the old broken wall in the garden; little

Freddy in front of the others, with their hands out. Billy said they were very good and stood quite still until the Master had finished. Mr P. P. was so pleased with them he'd given them a whole sixpence between them!

Mam was glad to have that picture, though she always said it was a shame it had been taken when the children looked so peaky and that Billy should never have taken them out with the old garden-play sacks on.

Some time after that Mrs Atts was tidying up the parlour. 'Here,' she calls, 'ain't these some o' your lot?'

A parcel had come that morning with a big book in it. I'd seen the Missus unpacking it. '*The Almanack*,' she says to Mr P. P. It was a dark green book with gold printing on it and gold edges to the pages. It didn't half glitter when she lifted it out!

Mrs Atts had the book on the table. I went and

63

looked. Though it wasn't done the same way as the photo the Master had given me mam, being book-printed like, it was Ours all right. Three little thin kids with sacks round their shoulders, and their hands stretched out: Tottie, Phillie and little Freddy standing good and still.

'Can you read?' asks Mrs Atts.

'Not very well,' I says. So she does it for me. I'll never forget what she read. It was:

> *The London Beggar Children*
> *Are pleading in the street:*
> *'Spare but a farthing, sir,' they cry*
> *To each unheeding passer-by*
> *'Oh, would you see us children die*
> *For want of bread to eat?'*

'That ain't *true*,' I says. 'He gave 'em sixpence but they never begged. He said it was extra for standing still.' I was so upset I could have cried.

'He don't mean it personal. It's what they call artistical licence,' Mrs Atts tells me.

Now old Fanny Atts might have been a dirty old party who scamped the work and liked her drop of gin, but she had a heart of gold. 'Look,' she says, 'it's between you and me, see? It's not likely anyone we know is going to set eyes on a fancy book like this one. So what say we keep quiet? No need to shame your good ma and pa, is there?'

I said no, and I didn't tell anyone. Not even Billy. Not that I didn't trust him but I was afraid he might have sorted me Master out for letting such lies appear about our family.

Only Mrs Atts and me knew, and she never let on either.

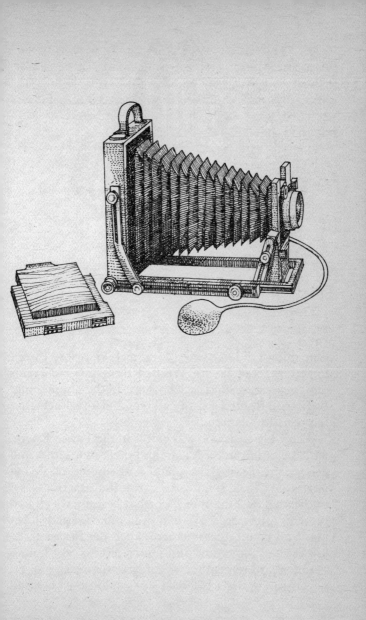

TREATS

One thing I did like when I was a child, before I went to service, was Treats. We had three or four Treats most years, the Sunday School one in the summer and the Parish Room Christmas Treat and any others that happened to come up.

The Christmas one was carols in the Parish Room, with a word from the Vicar, and then some ladies and gentlemen playing the piano and singing or saying poetry. We liked singing the carols, but the rest was a bit beyond us. Still, it was worth it because we all had presents afterwards. We had things like knitted stockings and comforters and red calico needlecases. We always had some nuts and mince pies to take home.

One year I remember we got an orange each too. I'd never seen oranges before. I just couldn't get over all them round, golden balls heaped up by the piano with bits of holly tucked in here and there. All the kids were whispering and pointing. 'There's one each,' someone said. I don't know how I got through waiting for that concert to end.

Some of the kids ate their oranges on the way home – peel and all; but we didn't (there were four of us then) we took them home for our mam along with the mince pies and the nuts.

I remember us running down the road that evening. It was frosty and misty and there were little fiery sparks when the nails on Billy's boots hit the ground. We held them golden oranges up in the air as we ran, and now and again we'd just stop in our tracks to smell them. I always take a sniff at an orange afore I peels it, even now – it's such a lovely bitterish smell.

Anyway, when we gets home mam (who knew about oranges having been in genteel service) sent me and Billy out to Mr Webb-on-the-Corner's shop for a ha'porth of *re*fined sugar. That caused some excitement straight away for we'd never seen any but the strong brown, and that not too often.

The next day being Sunday we all stood around, even dad – while mam peeled them four oranges and broke them apart. We'd never seen anything but the insides of apples and pears before, and them little purses all packed with juice made us shout aloud for pleasure. Then mam rolled the pieces in the *re*fined sugar (which is white and powdery-like) and laid them all out on her best china dish and set them in the larder to soak up the sugar.

As for the peel, that was put on a flat tin on the rack over the kitchen cooker so it could dry slowly. It dried for some days and kept the kitchen smelling lovely right over Christmas. When it was all crisp and withered mam broke it up and put it in a stone crock and used a pinch now and then to flavour a baking of hard pears or a batch of oat cakes.

But oh! The excitement of eating them sugared orange bits. We sucked them slowly and our hands got sticky. When we finished we ran our fingers round the dish and sucked the orangey sugar off them.

But, as I was saying: Treats! I recollect a Treat by the river with fireworks and baked potatoes when one of the gentry's nephews rowed in a winning boat team. Sometimes we had 'lection Treats, when someone had got into Parliament, with toffee apples for us, and beer for the grown-ups, but Sunday School Treats were the best by far.

We always had Sunday School Treats in the summer, in the garden of one of the big houses backing on the river. There'd be a big tent in case it rained, and long board tables with plates of bread-and-jam sandwiches, cut cake, buns, biscuits and slices of cheese on them, and a china wash-bowl full of radishes and lettuce leaves and half-tomatoes in the middle. It wasn't half a tuck-in!

I remember we used to sit down to tea on them sort of nasty chairs you don't see so much of nowadays – very dangerous ones that folded up sudden so you *could* nip your fingers off if you weren't lively. (Not that I remember anyone actually losing a finger, but it always added to the excitement to know it could happen.)

This Treat was for the kids who went to the Church Sunday School. The Chapels had Treats too, but nothing like so good as ours. The Chapel kids used to stand outside the big house to watch us go in and then hang about outside listening. We would make a great deal of noise, just to make them jealous, like, 'o–o–o–ooh', when they brought more cakes in, and 'hooray' when we'd finished eating.

All the food was sent in by the people from the genteel families who went to our church. Good, nice plain stuff and plenty of it. They sent their servants to help too and it made us feel very rich having our mugs filled up by maids in white aprons.

Some of the big boys would call, 'More, more!' when a plate was empty, but our family never did. We knew it was very rude.

After tea we ran races, and gentlemen took us for a row up the river, or got the boys doing tug-o'-war. Before we went home we took a dip in a bran tub for little presents wrapped in pink paper. I remember I once got a little 'broidered thing full of hairpins, and our Charlie had a lady's cardcase with the lock broke off. I suppose they'd been sent in by ladies who didn't want them any longer –like for rummage sales nowadays. Still, we were grateful, it was so nice getting any-thing!

Now, I've been telling you about my childhood Treats, but do you know, a time came, when I was ten years old and grown out of such pleasures, that I found myself on the dishing-up side of the picture as it were. I was working at the time for a nice young lady whose regular maid was laid up at a London Hospital for an operation. This young lady – do you know I've forgot her name? – lent me to go over and help at the Treat. She got her Cook to make a lovely lot of pink cakes. Pink – inside and out! With icing and a real fresh raspberry pushed into the icing on every one of them. There had never been such cakes at any of the Treats I'd ever remembered.

The cook let me help her with the icing, and the raspberries.

'Ah,' says this cook, 'the Missus means well – bless her nice heart, but I reckon it's unlikely as any of our young Sunday-scholars'll get as much as a sniff of these-here.'

And she told me that after the Treat was over, the things that were left were given to the Verger's wife to make up into parcels for the poor old folk of the town, and that she, and three other women looked to the unpacking of goodies that came in from the big houses, and regularly set aside anything that particularly took their fancies for themselves. Cook said she knew this was a fact because her cousin who worked for the Hamphreys, where there was a Frenchy cook, had recognised a most elegant cake that only that cook could have made on the Verger's wife's sideboard. It was a cake that Cook's cousin knew had been a left-over from a Hamphrey's party of two nights back!

'Have *you* ever seen say, a chocolate cake or an almond fancy or even a frosted apple-cake at one of them Treats?' Cook says. 'Well, I know for a fact that such has been sent in in the past from kitchens around.'

I hadn't seen anything like that. 'Mind you,' I tells her, 'what we've had has been really lovely.'

Cook said, 'It should have been lovelier,' and then she said I'd better taste how lovely the pink cakes was while they were still going. So I ate one, and it was really beautiful.

'Don't the ladies and gentlemen at the Treat notice

70

that things are missing?' I said.

'They have their tea at the same time as the children. They takes it in the drawing-room,' Cook says. 'It helps to get their strength up before they tackle the games and things.'

When I carried the box full of cakes round to the Treat that afternoon I could have cried to think that me brothers and sisters wouldn't get a chance to taste them. I was sorry for the other kids too. It just wasn't fair.

Now, I'm not like some. I'll sit down under a lot, but fair's fair I always say. Anyway, I didn't go straight into the big house. I sat down for a minute on a bench in the shrubbery and had a little think. There was a sort of grotto-place in the shrubbery made of rock-work and I went and hid that box of cakes in there, on the floor behind some big stones where it couldn't be seen. Then I went on to the house and helped spread the jam on the bread and cut up the cakes and did as I was bid, meek as a mouse.

I kept my eyes open though, and I saw Cook wasn't far out. The Verger's wife was there all right, and so were her friends. Very busy giving things out and telling folk what to do. Sometimes though, she'd open a box, or peek into a basket, and there'd be a nod to one of her cronies and whatever was in the basket or box would be whisked away into a closet.

Oh, it did feel strange to be showing those Treat children to their places, settling the little ones up on boat-cushions so's they could reach the table, and making sure the big boys weren't sitting together. I looked over to where me Billy and our other children were sitting, I saw their little shiny-clean faces, and their new-washed clothes, and it made me feel a hundred years old. Last year I'd been happily eating with them instead of filling up mugs and handing round buns.

When you're not eating yourself, watching other people is interesting. My goodness, those children did pack it away! Presently the big boys started up, 'MORE, MORE, MORE,' and some of them banged the tables to make the Chapel kids mad.

'MORE, MORE, MORE, HOO-RAY,' they went.

'Go and fetch some more,' says Mrs Verger to me. So I did. Only I didn't go to the kitchen for buns. I went for a big tray I'd seen on the dresser there. Then I went round to the rockwork grotto to get that box of pink cakes.

I was having a bit of a struggle – it's always harder getting things out than it is putting them in when you've chosen an awkward place – and I didn't want to up-end the box and damage the cakes, in fact, I'd got to a state when I couldn't put the box down and move one of them big stones at the same time, when someone says, very polite, 'May I help you?'

It made me jump so I wonder I didn't drop the lot. I looks over me shoulder, and there's a nice young gentleman – about fourteen I'd have said, and a younger Miss. Brother and sister, I'd have reckoned – they looked alike.

'I'm trying to get this out without spoiling the cakes,' I says. 'If you could move this rock it would be fine.'

So the young Nob moves the rock aside and I gets me box out easy. I got up, a bit cobwebby after all that scrabbling, and the young Miss helps me dust meself down.

They told me they'd been hiding behind the tea-tent listening to the row, when they saw me go off to the kitchen. 'You looked so mysterious, we thought you were up to something,' they tells me. Anyway, they followed me and it was as well they did.

Those two were very interested in the box, so I let them have a peep at the cakes and told them why I'd hid them. It's funny – I'd rather have died than tell any grown-up gentry about the Verger's wife's art-fulness, but seeing these two were but children it came quite natural to speak out. I told them about the cakes that got put aside and everything. When I let on what I had a mind to do they were with me at once.

'That's capital!' they says. 'We're with you.'

So then I took the lid right off the box and the young Miss helped me put the pink cakes on the kitchen tray. The young gent carried the tray round to the tent for me, and then he and the Miss scampered off. 'We'll see you again,' they says as they runs.

The children were all tucking in, but when they saw me walking in with all that iced pinkiness in front of me, they started to shout and bang as if they had been starved for weeks and couldn't wait to get at them raspberry tops! You should have seen the faces of Billy and the rest when they took theirs. 'They're good,' I says, 'I've tasted.'

I don't know if it was because there happened to be so many big boys in the Sunday School that year, but I don't think there'd ever been such a din at a Treat before. They hollered so loud that the noise was took up by the Chapel kids outside who hollered back as if they had gone mad with jealousy.

I didn't look at the Verger's wife once as I took me tray round the tables. I just acted meek as if it was the most usual thing in the world to be handing out goodies she hadn't even seen.

There was an even louder row next though. For what do you think had happened? That young Sir and Miss had gone back to the kitchen and opened up the closet and taken out all the Verger's wife's hoard of goodies and put them out for the maids to cut up and bring round, and the maids, who were only too glad to do so, came in grinning, with dish-loads of special things.

I am glad our lot minded their manners and remembered not to grab and to say, 'thank you', but some of those Sunday School kids gobbled and guzzled until it was a wonder they didn't burst asunder. How some of them managed to run in the races or tug on the ropes after that tea I can't think. Still, in spite of all that pigging, there was still more than enough left over for the poor old people. I was very glad about that because old people do like sweet things and they don't often get a chance to taste them.

When the tea was over, I helped the other maids to clear the table and wash the dirty crocks. I was going over the grass to collect some more mugs for washing, when I heard a lot of loud cheering coming from outside the garden wall. It was so wild I just had to nip along to the gate and have a look out to see what was up.

It was them Chapel kids hollering and cheering, because a shower of buns and cakes were coming over the wall at them. I went back in again, and was just in time to see that saucy young Sir and Miss running through the bushes, laughing fit to bust themselves. I had to laugh too. For once in a while the Chapel kids had done nearly as well as our lot.

Later on I saw the young Sir and Miss again standing very prim and quiet by the gentleman who was giving out the sports prizes. They looked very meek and tidy. The young gent looked across and saw me, but he didn't so much as raise an eyebrow. If I hadn't known better I'd have said them two would have had a job to swallow butter, for it looked as if it would never have melted in *their* mouths.

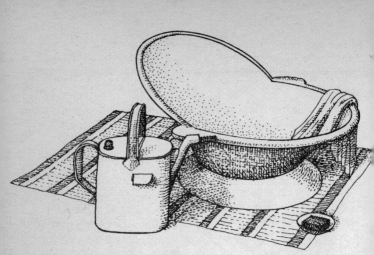

THE DAY ACADEMY FOR
YOUNG LADIES

As you know, I didn't have much schooling; but I can
still remember what school was like; all them children
sitting bolt upright in rows and the maps and the Doh-
Ray-Me cards and the big cane hung up where everyone could see them. And quiet! There wasn't an unto-
ward sound. Just a squeak from a slate pencil and the
drim-drone of tables and spellings, and the teacher's
voice and someone answering. (Our Tottie once said
that school was like a strict church and I think she was
about right.)

I used to think all schools were like that until I did a
fill-in at a Young Lady's School. I got this place because they had a cook called Mrs Selby who knew me
mam. She was a nice dark-faced woman with white
frizzy hair whose husband had been a sailor drowned

at sea, and she often came to see us.

Mrs Selby said I'd only be wanted till the end of the school term when they'd have time to look for someone older.

Mam hemmed and ha'd a bit, and I could see there was something she didn't like about the idea, but Mrs Selby said I'd be all right with her so she gave in.

The school which called itself a Day Academy for Young Ladies was the end one of a row of houses that used to be in Strawberry Vale. It was a steep old place of four floors, most of them given over to the schooling. There were some twenty young misses between eight and eighteen years old split into two classes; one in the downstairs front room and the other in the two rooms above made into one with the folding doors pushed back.

There were two tiny little orphan sisters too, who were brought and fetched by an old servant woman. They sat in a poky little room next to the kitchen, making O's and pot-hooks on lined paper, with their clean hankies pinned to their bodices and their little legs dangling – all eyes and yawns poor little mites. But good as gold, not a bit like the big young ladies who were a terribly noisy lot.

The classrooms and stairs had bare wood floors and those misses clattered and clumped about in their light boots in a way that would have had our old teacher reaching for the tickle-toby. (And our lot wore hobnails which are hard to go quiet in.)

Them young ladies chattered and giggled and answered back in class in the cheekiest way. The teachers were two thin old maidens called the Misses Drapers and these old dears and another living-in mistress called Miss Rose were always clapping their hands

79

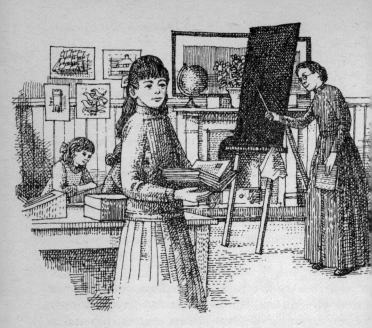

and saying, 'Young ladies, young ladies, less noise *please,*' without it making the slightest difference.

'They ought to have a swiffy cane here,' I says to Mrs Selby. 'Just the sight of it would be enough to hush them girls up.'

Mrs Selby told me that Academies weren't the same as free schools. She said this Academy was a cheap old place for jumped up people to send their kids to. So long as they could say they went private they didn't much care how the school was run.

I told me mam about that, and she said it was surprising the things people put first when it was a question of trying to be genteel. But she didn't believe in whacking children herself. And do you know, with ten of us in all, neither Mam nor Dad ever had cause to beat any of us.

Mrs Selby did take care of me. She saw that I wasn't put on by anyone, and she dinned into me all the time to keep clear of the young misses, just speak when spoken to and no more. 'Don't bandy words with them,' she says, 'For some of them ain't nice.'

Well, I certainly didn't speak to them if I could help it, but gracious, some of them were my own age, and it was only natural I should listen to their babble, especially at dinner-time when those who didn't live near enough to go home ate in the downstairs dining-room where I helped serve the food.

Them young misses had crazes about things. They sat at tables in their classrooms, with brass hooks screwed to the table sides for them to hang their work-bags and their nets of books. When I was working there they had a fashion for each miss to have her own writing box that opened out to a slanting top and a place to hold pens and two natty little inkpots which she kept on her table. I heard so much about them boxes while I was handing round the potatoes I just had to go and pay me tuppence!

I had no call to go into them classrooms at all, they were scrubbed at night by a by-the-hour woman, but I'd heard so much boasting and comparing of boxes I nipped up for a look one day while the girls were exercising after lunch, which meant they walked round and round the little lawn and up and down the paths.

Anyways, I had a good look round, and I must say some of them boxes were a bit of all right. There was one made of wood that smelt lovely with white ivory bits let into the lid in patterns, and another covered in maroon plush with brass corners and handles that I'd have given my ears for. The one I'd heard most boasting about was one made of green morocco leather with a solid silver clasp, belonging to a nasty young miss called Emily Rush. It didn't take me long to spot that one! It was supposed to be the most valuable box of all, but give me the plush, I thought!

Now, I'd been told to keep clear of the young ladies, but it didn't mean they kept clear of me given the chance. The three teachers slept in bedrooms on the third floor that I had to keep tidy. When I'd done them for the day I had to lock them up and hang the keys in the kitchen cupboard. I suppose that was to keep the young misses from poking about and discovering secrets, for the three upstairs attics were given over to pianos and the young ladies were up and down at all hours, thumping and tinkling and banging as it suited them and they had to cross the bedroom landing to go upstairs. If one of them heard me moving about in one of the rooms the door knob would start rattling and someone would be trying to lure me out for a chat.

I kept them doors bolted from inside though. I didn't trust them girls and their chats. Especially the big ones. That one called Miss Emily Rush was really nasty. Once she caught me by the apron down in the front hall and said, 'Now, you mouse, what are *you* afraid of?' And she said it in such a spiteful way I thought she meant mischief.

I may be little but I'm not easily scared. 'I'm afraid of me dad,' I says quick. 'He eats big young ladies like you for breakfast, so don't go walking up our way.'

Some of the youngest misses tittered, but that Miss Rush didn't. 'I can handle rude little servant girls,' she says, 'So you'd better look out.'

After that some of the young ladies really tried to get round me. (I don't think they liked that Miss Rush much.) They gave me lots of smiles and nods and friendly words, but I kept my distance. Except with them little tiny girls in the back-room, Mrs Selby had made little pets of them. They were so good and scared and so often left to themselves. Miss Rose would pop in and set them a copy or tack the sides of a couple of dusters for them to stitch, and then go off to oversee the piano-playings and such, and there they'd be: cut off from the rest of the school with only Mrs Selby and me to give an eye to them.

Mrs Selby slept at the school too. Her room was on the same floor as the teachers – a small one at the back, but she did her own tidying. I didn't sleep in though. They'd wanted me to, but Mam had said 'no' to that, our Charlie would walk me over in the mornings and meet me in the evenings. Was I glad! The servant I'd took over from had slept in a little spidery wash-house behind the kitchen on a camp bed that had to be folded up on Wash-day. I much preferred going home and wriggling into the big bed among me young sisters.

That last servant had gone mad all of a sudden and been rushed off to the Lunatic House on the town stretcher-on-wheels with the canvas cover. Mam must have known about it, though she hadn't told me. I picked it up from one of the young ladies.

As well as me regular housework, I often had to run to the Post-Office or take messages. One day, when one of the young ladies had a headache I had to walk her home. She was older and bigger than me so I don't know what I'd have done if she'd fainted. But she didn't, she got quite cheerful by the time we got to the place where she lived. She gave me a paper full of toffee

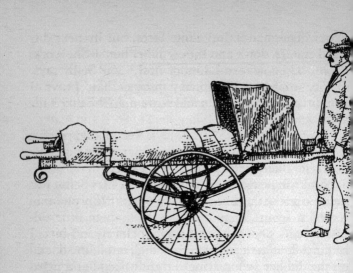

lumps from inside her muff and a halfpenny from her pocket and said she'd begun to feel better the minute she left school.

This was the young lady who told me about the mad servant. She told me the poor woman had shrieked all the way to Kingston. She seemed to think it was very funny. I couldn't see it that way meself, and when I got back I said as much to Mrs Selby.

Mrs Selby said, 'How lies spread!' She said that young woman hadn't been mad at all. Just frightened silly. There'd been a lot of ghostly talk from the girls and the poor thing took it in.

'I think one of them must have played some sort of trick. She was very strung up because of what the girls had said about ghosts in the house,' Mrs Selby tells me. 'Then, one late afternoon, she saw something that upset her, and she had high stericks and couldn't stop. She did seem mad, and they did take her off, shouting about black hands and white faces, but by next day she'd calmed down and they sent her home. She works down the Snowflake Laundry now,' Mrs Selby says.

'I bet that Miss Rush had a hand in that,' I says. 'I expect she thought she could scare me. She asked me what I was afraid of.'

'I think so too,' said Mrs Selby. 'And all them girls is under her thumb – even them as hates her.'

'Well, I keep out of her way,' I said.

Now, all the time this was going on, Mrs Selby was being kinder and kinder to them poor little orphans in the back room. Sometimes she made them little tid-bits to eat. She used to make up lovely tid-bits. I remember once she cut some fingers of bread and dipped them in melted butter and treacle and dried them crisp at the back of the oven in a way I've never been able to copy since, though I've often tried. As for me – I used to pop in now and again and tell them the latest tales about the goings-on of my brothers and sisters. They liked that.

Although it wasn't supposed to be my task I used to take the little things up to the water-closet and help them on to the seat which was very high for them, and I always got them into their cloaks and bonnets when it was time for them to be taken home. Every day they went in to kiss Mrs Selby before they went, and they always kissed me at the front door.

One day when they were kissing me good-bye that Miss Rush was coming out with one of her best friends. She said, 'Disgusting! Fancy being kissed by a filthy little slavey. You shouldn't allow it,' she said to the old servant. But the old girl didn't take no notice of her. She said, 'A jumped up poppycock, that one.' And I said, 'Yes.'

And then that Miss Rush did a mean and spiteful thing. She got at them poor little orphans. She started to tease and worry them. In the dinner-time, when the poor little things would be trotting down the path for exercise, she'd start nagging at them. It wasn't ordinary nagging either. Just sort of creepy and nasty.

This didn't come out till afterwards, though some of the girls knew what was going on. Of course, Mrs Selby and I didn't know about this. We only noticed the little things were getting quieter and peakier.

The little girls lived with an auntie and uncle who were very fond of them, and one day one of the children fell down the back coal-house steps, when they should have been walking round the garden. They had been hiding in the coal-house to keep out of Miss Rush's way. When they got home that day their auntie got the whole story out of them and there was a terrible uproar and they were taken away from the school.

Nothing happened to that Miss Rush, which made me mad. Mrs Selby said, 'Losing two lots of school fees the old ladies can't afford to lose any more.'

I thought of those timid little mites and I thought of that poor servant who'd been frightened and my blood boiled. Mrs Selby said there was nothing I could do, but I knew she was very sorry about those little ones going.

As I said, I was only there to the end of the term. The last day the young ladies would take their workbags and their nets of books and their writing boxes home and the school be left to the cleaners and the menders.

Mrs Selby was very sad for her. 'I'll miss making them tasty bits for them babies,' she said. 'They specially liked me treacle tid-bits.'

And then I did a very wicked thing. While the girls

were having their last exercise round the garden, I sneaked upstairs to the big classroom with something under me apron.

As I say, that was my last day at that school. Mrs Selby left soon after too, so she could never tell me anything. I should like to know what that Miss Rush thought when she got home and opened her morocco leather box. I reckon that treacle must have taken some removing.

A BIT OF HIGH LIFE

You mightn't believe it, but there was a time when I was young when I worked for a titled family. Oh yes; only temporary, but still, it means I can say I saw a bit of high life.

It came about like this. When I was a little kid I'd been rather taken up and petted by a big girl called Dora who lived down near the church. She used to hump me about and pretend I was her baby, and take me in the park to pick harebells and bring me back to her mam's place to wash me face and curl me hair and give me sugar-bup to eat. (Sugar-bup? – that's bread and butter with brown sugar sprinkled on it.)

Dora went off into service a couple of years before our Edie was born, and I was very cut up about it. Not being any handier with a pen than I was, it meant I never heard direct from her as to how she was getting on. Only bits of news from my mam who got it from Dora's mam now and again.

It seemed Dora was over to Esher with a real high-up family. A Sir and a Lady with two young ladies and a young gentleman away at boarding school. Not much money, is what Dora's mam thought. Only four servants, and what's to spare spent in outward show, but mean and penny-pinching behind the scenes. Which meant meagre food and pay for the servants every time.

Now things were always hard in our family, but what we had we shared, and what we hadn't got we didn't mind our neighbours knowing about, but it appears hard-upness is a shame and disgrace to gentry and they'll do anything to hide it from their friends.

Poor feeding must have come hard to Dora, for having been the youngest in her family with two working brothers at home, she had never been so near the bone as we were. There had always been a knuckle of meat in the pot and a cloth pudding to follow on their table, as I remember.

I said I wondered Dora's mam didn't fetch her home like I'd been fetched from the Miss Gooches, but Mam said, oh no, that Dora was lucky to have got in with an entitled family. A few steady years with such behind her, and a tidy reference, and she'd have the pick and choosing of a good situation anywhere. For lesser, though richer gentlefolk, liked to have someone from a titled family working in their homes. Mam said even the well-off commoners were curious about high life.

I thought about that and saw how it could be. I'd never seen a Sir or Lady in my life, though I'd heard of such, and I must say I was curious about such high gentlefolk, even if they was down on their luck. It struck me that if I had chance of a word with Dora I'd turn her inside out to find out in what ways they were different from people like us.

Mam said it was blue blood. But she wasn't right there. Their blood's the same colour as ours, I looked special when I had the chance. And this is how it happened.

One of the times when I was home and beginning to look around for another temporary living in place, Dora's mam came trundling down the lane making for our gate with a message from Dora.

It seemed that one of the maids at her place had had to go home in a hurry because her mother was took sick, and they was wanting someone to fill in for a while 'till she got back. Dora had thought of me being home and had mentioned it to the Lady. The Lady said if my references were good she would take me on.

There was an excitement for you! So, after a letter to her Ladyship from our young Mrs Vicar, off I went, on a bright May morning with the straw box and bundle before me, in *The Angler*'s pony-and-trap driven by *The Angler*'s pot-boy – bowling along through Bushey Park between all the chestnut trees in bloom, through Molesey and Thames Ditton, where there used to be fields full of brown cows and yellow buttercups, to the Sir and Lady's place at Esher.

I don't know what I thought a Sir's place would look like, but this one wasn't anything very special. Just a wide old-fashioned front with mauve flowers growing all over it, and windows made of spikey panes of glass in patterns.

As we drove in, I sees someone up a step-ladder

polishing one of them spiky panes, and I was just thinking what a fiddly job it must be to clean windows like that, when the person looks round, and it's Dora!

I wouldn't hardly have known that Dora, she'd grown so tall and spindly, and so quiet, but very glad to see me. It seemed the ladies were out visiting somewhere, and the Sir was upstairs not to be disturbed, so Dora could take me in to meet the other servants in peace.

There was a cook and a housemaid as well as Dora. There was also a man called Mr Latterby who came in twice a week for the garden. There was a boy too whose name was Rob; he was Mr Latterby's son, who helped his dad sometimes. Rob came in for an hour every morning to clean the boots and the knives and sift the cinders and fill the coal-scuttles. Mr Latterby worked in other people's gardens the rest of the time, but Rob went to school whenever he could. It seemed that Rob was quite a scholar – afterwards I heard he passed to be a schoolmaster in Hampshire.

The servants seemed a worried and nervous lot – all soft-speaking, except Rob. He didn't seem to care for nothing, that boy. Dora took me over the house to show me me duties, and she seemed so anxious everything should be just so, and nothing wasted, I began to feel quite depressed. I might even have thought about running off home if it hadn't been for that Rob.

Dora had been showing me all the bars of hard soap laid out in the laundry and telling me we always had to use the hardest bits first, and was just coming out into the garden again when she says, 'Oh, and in the hall-cupboard there's a pile of newspapers for the parlour carpet. We spread them over the carpet so it won't fade when the sun shines. We take them up for company, and put them back when the callers have gone.'

'What happens if someone comes unexpected?' I has to say.

'Milady plops down on the floor and pretends she's cutting out paper-patterns for petticoats for the poor,' says a voice, and it's that Rob, laughing his head off.

'Does she?' I asks and Dora shakes her head. 'You'll get into trouble one of these days, Robert,' she says. 'Then your father will be put off.'

'He could always get something better,' says Rob. 'He's a good gardener. It's only that he likes to say he's working for titled folk. And don't my lady know it.'

And that's when I learned something else. It seemed that some servants preferred to be with titles – even if the pay wasn't that good. Not like Dora, to get a reference and move on to a better place, but just to be around with the Nobs, like Mr Latterby.

Just then the Lady and the Missesses came back from their visit and I had to be brought in for them to look at me. Lor! Wasn't I disappointed. I don't know what I expected to see really.

On a nice Sunday afternoon when our dad walked us older children over to Hampton Court I'd seen traps and carriages full of nice brightly dressed people out for an airing, and because they'd looked so happy I suppose I'd thought that's what Sirs and Ladyships would look like. But not this lot.

The Sir turned out to be a mizzly old man who kept right out of everyone's way, and the Lady was very tart and snappy with a tongue like cold poison. As for the Missesses (and one of them no older than me) they turned out to be a miserable pair with 'nothing to do and all day to do it in' as they say; hanging about the drawing-room with a bit of needlework or a dab of painting to fall back on. I wondered how they stood it. And great black pinnies up to their chins to whip off if anyone called.

That place was all pinnies and coverings-up. Even the chairs and sofas had covers drawed over them to save the real coverings from being used. It was covers off and covers on all the time. 'If that's high-up living it's not for me,' I says to meself.

And everyone took it all so solemn. The Lady's eyes were everywhere, looking for waste of money in everything. If you stood a minute to look out of a window she drove you off to another task. If Cook sent in more than six potatoes to a meal she wanted to know why.

Rob told me no one daren't shake the tablecloth out for the birds without measuring the crumbs first to see if they'd do to make bread-pudding with. Of course, he was joking, but I saw what he meant and had a right old giggle.

It was different though when visitors were expected. Then all sorts of fancy china and glass came to light and nice stiff tablecloths for the table and sideboard. You never saw such a conjuring trick. Lots of good tasty dishes and the Sir and Lady done up to the nines. Dora told me that if they had a dinner party they sometimes got Mr Latterby to dress up like a waiter to help at table.

We were in the kitchen when she told me that. I was shelling peas and Rob was scraping the knives up and down the stone and setting my teeth on edge, I remember. 'Oh yes,' he says, 'And then it's Latterby's nectarines or Latterby's grapes and my silly old father is flattered to think how much his hard-grown produce is appreciated.'

I asked Rob later on what he was getting at, and he

told me. His dad made a bit extra growing fruit in some greenhouses behind their cottage. Very fine fruit it seems that he got a good price for from the best greengrocers. It seemed my lady had got into the way of buttering him up about his fruit so's he'd give her some gladly, as a sort of humble gift, when he really should be selling it to help support his family.

'Every time there's to be a special meal laid on, it's all smiles and hints and Mr Latterby's,' says Rob, 'And my silly old dad falls for it. The best fruit too, mind you – for nothing but a bit of condescension and the chance to hear it praised while he's passing round the dishes.'

I liked the way that Rob went on. It cheered me up, specially when I was feeling extra hungry and tired.

Then something happened just before I left that I'll never forget as long as I live.

It seemed some very high-up folk was coming to have a dinner with the Sir and Ladyship. The son of these high folks had given a bit of an eye to the eldest young Miss and from what I picked up in the kitchen – where they seemed to know everything – it was being hoped that a marriage might be in the offing. As it happened, nothing came of their hopes, and I still wonder if it could have been different if it hadn't been for Rob.

The day these people were due to come, we were up to our necks in work. Dora and the housemaid and I were kept polishing and cleaning. There were some bits of silver brought up in bags from the cellar; candlesticks and dishes and spoons and forks with great square handles that I hadn't seen before, to be rubbed with pink polish. The Lady went out in the garden to snip flowers because it wasn't Mr Latterby's day – he was coming to wait at table later on – and the young

Misses were curling each other's hairs with hot tongs, and sewing lavender bags into their camisoles!

Now I was seeing high-life all right. You should have smelt the kitchen! 'I could eat the steam,' I tells Rob. And he says, 'That's about all you're likely to get, so make the most of it.'

Then suddenly things took a bad turn. First the Sir tore one of his ruffles and Dora had to sit down and mend it just when she'd got her hands full with setting out the drawing-room ornaments. Then Cook said the beef smelt offish. And then Rob came in with a long face to say poor Mr Latterby had got a racking head from having been working in the sun all day, and was took sick with it and couldn't come and wait at table after all! You should have heard the Lady!

No poor old Mr Latterby nor nothing! Just, 'It's too bad. Latterby should have been more careful. Fancy standing about in the sun when he knew we were relying on him for tonight!'

I thought, if that's what Ladyships were like I wouldn't want any more of them. As for Rob he began to get red as fire, and I could see he was mad. But he managed not to say anything. He was just turning to go when the Lady says, 'And the grapes? Mr Latterby promised me some grapes.'

If I'd been Rob I think I'd ha' said, 'Buy some for a change,' but he just went off without a word.

You should have heard that Lady. My mam used to say when I got wild and shouted that I wasn't being ladylike. I could tell her that some ladies weren't either.

Dora said they could manage without Mr Latterby, if I could run between the kitchen and dining-room with the dishes, and the cook said she could see me half-way in case of spills, but even then the Lady was wild.

She went on and on about the Latterbys – how unreliable they were and how she'd only taken Rob for odd jobs out of charity – and that wasn't true because Rob worked really hard.

The young ladies had just come down with their curls in place and their white dresses on when Rob comes back in time to catch some of the Lady's nasty remarks. He had a dish with a great big bunch of dark blue grapes on it. I've never seen such monsters. 'My father got up to pick these for you, my lady,' he says, and he looks straight at her. 'They were the best he had.'

You'd have thought that Lady would have been ashamed. But not a bit, not her. She looks at them lovely grapes and she says, 'They're dusty. Hadn't you the sense to dip and hang them before you brought them?'

Rob went all white round his nose with temper, but he says, 'I'll do it at once, my lady,' and off he goes, and because I didn't know what dip and hang meant I followed him. It means dipping them in water and then pegging them on the line to dry. The weather was hot so it didn't take long.

Now, I didn't say a word to anyone about how Rob dipped them grapes. I just went and fetched them when I was told to and put them on the silver dish on the sideboard.

Well, the company came and sat down to their dinner, and I rushed from kitchen to dining-room and back and scrooped a finger round a dish before I put it back in the pantry, for hasty lick on the way back, I can tell you.

The meat had been offish but Cook had covered the taste with spices, and the jellies was softish, but them grapes on the sideboard looked lovely and cool when Dora put them on the table.

Gentry have special scissors to cut grapes. They snip off little branches and put them on their plates, and then they eat them. When that lot started on those grapes you should have heard the uproar. They must have tasted awful. You see, they had a sort of greeny sliminess dried among them, and worse than that, when the Sir broke his bunch apart a tiny little dead goldfish dropped out on to his plate. The biggest

Miss was so upset she cut her little finger on them grape scissors and it bled terrible. That's how I know gentry's blood was the same colour as anyone else's.

I knew what that Rob had done, because I'd seen him do it. He'd been so wild with the Lady he'd just swooshed those grapes in the goldfish pond down the garden. It hadn't rained for days so the pond was all slimy.

I went home two days after so I didn't see how it ended. I know Rob didn't come in next day. I heard the housemaid say he'd got a morning job at the butcher's sweeping out the sawdust and washing down the meat-blocks. She said he would get twice as much money and a bit of meat now and again too. I don't know if Mr Latterby ever went back to work there, I forgot to ask. I hope he didn't.

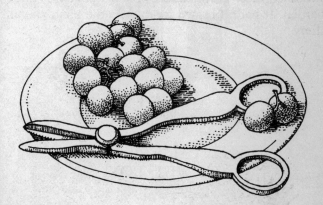

THE TALE OF THE
USEFUL BOY

It was bad enough being a girl and going out to work in service when I was young but it was much worse for boys. Not of course for boys in high-up situations – our mam's brother had gone in as a boots-and-knife boy to a Big House and ended up as a Lordship's Butler – but boys as went in as 'Usefuls' in an ordinary household. They weren't trained for much, and when they got bigger and their appetites grew they were paid off and someone else took their place. Usually they were taken on for Charity.

There was a boy like that in the place next door to my Miss Johnson. The people who lived there had two of them joined-together surnames: Scott-Browning I think it was, though I might have misremembered. Anyway, they had a big house and garden with an apple-and-pear orchard between us and them. All the houses were built on the slope of a hill, and us being above them, we could look over our garden wall right on to the orchard tree-tops.

These Scott-Brownings had a living-in girl too. She was about my age, a squatty dark thing called Ethel who was afraid of her shadow, and this boy, Mason they called him, who hardly lived-in because he bedded down in the mouldy hay on top of the stable where there used to be a horse. (Mr and Mrs Scott-Browning didn't have a horse, no more did my Miss Johnson: when they wanted to be driven anywhere they sent a note down to the cab rank by the station.)

When I first went to Miss Johnson's I thought I was in Heaven. I thought she was such a nice *old* dear – all of forty-five she must have been then – a deal younger than I am now, but I thought she was very ancient! Mind you, could I be blamed when ladies over forty dressed like Charlie's Aunties, in blacks and dark browns and wore caps with lappets and mittens all day long?

She was sprightly too. Tended her little garden, and gave a real hand with the housework and talked to me as if I was as good as she was. She'd been a governess once and travelled overseas with her people. She told me a lot about foreign lands. She'd been to a place where the streets were water and people went up and down in long thin boats like we went in cabs and to somewhere where all the houses had been buried in cinders when a mountain had blowed up, that people had dug out again with all the bits and pieces of crockery and such; and plaster effigies of the people who'd burned there laid out like a poppy-show. Very interesting it all was.

Miss Johnson gave me a little brooch made out of tiny bits of coloured stones called mosaic and a painting called the Blue Grotto that she'd done herself when she was in foreign parts. She wanted to give me some reading and writing lessons too, but I dodged away from that. I said, 'Please 'um, I think you'd just be wasting your time 'um – because I'm naturally *opaque*.'

I didn't know what 'opaque' meant, but I'd once heard a young gentleman telling a friend that someone was opaque when he meant muddle-headed – it was a slang word of the time I think. Miss Johnson laughed herself nearly sick about it and said well, if I was sure, she wouldn't worry me for she couldn't see any reason for hammering learning into happy heads that didn't need it. She said she'd done enough of that in her time. Thank heaven her auntie's money had made it so she didn't have to bother anymore!

Anyway – that's just to let you know how nice Miss Johnson was and give you an idea as to why I got so comfortable and at-home at her place, like we was real friends as well as people from different stations in life, and why when it came to helping that Mason next door when he was in trouble I turned to Miss Johnson.

At home we'd always been used to getting up early, so it was nothing for me to be around pegging out the mid-week wash at six o'clock of a summer's morning before me Miss was up. Sometimes, when I'd finished, I'd grab a crust of bread and butter and, holding it between me teeth, I'd shin up one of our fruit trees and sit on a branch and gnaw me vittles and look down a-top of all those green pears and apples in the Scott-Browningses' orchard. After that I might swing from me arms and drop down on to the path that was thick with moss; sometimes I'd lie on one of the broad branches with me legs up against the trunk, and rock meself and sing like a baby in its cradle or a dickeybird in its nest – showing me calico drawers and not caring because I thought there'd be no one around to see them.

That's how I came to speak to that Mason. For one morning I was just dropping down from me perch when I noticed that boy crouched low down under the orchard trees, gnawing away on a hard old green pear, and staring at me as if I was something strange the like of which he'd never seen before. This came as a shock, me thinking I had got the morning to meself, and knowing I had been behaving in a disrespectable way, I snapped at him sharp. 'Well,' I says, 'Did you get your eyeful? Paid your tuppence?' which was the way girls snapped at the young chaps who whistled when they showed their ankles when they climbed up off the paddle-steamer on a Saturday over Hampton Court.

But this boy didn't give a sarky answer, he just went on staring and his eyes got all wet and swimmy with tears as if he couldn't bear another nasty word from anyone in the world. So, instead of berating him further, I leaned over our wall and looked down on him where he was crouching.

'You'll get belly-ache if you eat them green things,' I says. 'Ain't you had breakfast?' And he shook his head. 'After they've ate,' he tells me and nods towards his master's house, 'I has what they leaves. I'm always hungry,' he says.

Then he tells me his name was Mason and about sleeping in the stable and that. He wasn't sure how old he was and he thought his other name was Dick.

'What about the girl?' I asked him. 'I've seen a girl

beating the carpet on them lines down there. Don't she give you anything?' Mason says no, sometimes that girl even eats some of his bits, she gets hungry too.

Now I had been in places where the food was pretty miserable and I'd been at Miss Ellum's where I'd gorged like a pig, but I'd never been given leavings. I knew if I had, our mam would have had me home quick.

I could see that Mason was as thin as a stick, and by his manner I could tell he was worried and frightened his Master and Missus would know he'd been complaining. He was afraid in case they sent him away, for in them days you might well starve to death without a job.

I said, 'Well, cheer up, mate,' and I told him how my Miss J. never minded how much I went into the

loaf at mealtimes. 'Look,' I says, 'I was going to butter myself another hunk with a dab of red jam to it, but instead, I'll give it to you if you like, so long as you promise not to tell a soul.' That way he could feel he'd got a secret over me as well as me having one over him, though I knew my Miss wouldn't have cared a bit if she knew.

So I spread the hunk of bread and the boy stood against the wall below and I dropped it into his hands and he took it back away under the trees and that was the last I saw of him for that morning.

He was there again the next morning though. This time he was a bit luckier, for Miss Johnson had had an old dear's tea-fight the afternoon before – three of her friends from Mortlake – and there had been some sandwiches and a morsel of cake over. 'Drop them in Mr Williamses' bucket next time you go down to the shop,' she tells me, 'There's not enough there to save, and anyway the bread would be hard by tomorrow.'

Mr Williams was the pork butcher, and there was a big bucket with a lid in his side-alley for pig-bits. People often left scraps in it. I thought, 'Well, that there Mason is a lot more deserving than pigs.' so I hid up the scraps and saved them for his breakfast. He grabbed them like they were silver and gold and pelted off with them and that's all I saw of him that day.

The next morning he was there and so was that Ethel – both of them – all eyes like starving sparrows. After that, I gave them our scraps, and now and again I'd lay out on a ha'penny bag of stales from the baker. In them days bakers used to sell off the day before's stale buns and things in the early morning before they opened shop. I'd let meself out dead early and be down by his yard-gate afore anyone else was stirring. I wonder now if he thought I was buying them for Miss J. because he used to give us some funny looks when we went by his shop.

The way them two kids ate! Once I left the porridge over the fire and it burned and Miss Johnson said to throw it away, and that Ethel and that Mason got through the whole lot.

Them Scott-Brownings were a fat old pair. Him especially – with one of them great big round fronts. On Sundays they had a job getting into church side-by-side they was so nourished-looking.

'I wonder you don't blow up at them,' I says to Mason. 'I'd want to upturn their dinners on their heads.'

Mason had a dry little laugh. '*She* does things to them sometimes,' he says and that Ethel nods.

'Spiders and beetles,' says Mason, 'mooshed up with a spoon and stirred into the hot-pot.'

'I bet you put her up to it,' I says, for I could see that Ethel was so beat and so squatty she'd never have thought of such an own-back as that.

But she must have been tough, that one, in spite of her low diet and the hard work – for apart from a cheap and drunken charwoman those two kids ran the housework – it was Mason who got frailer and frailer.

By winter he was light as a shadow and his face was all eyes, and he coughed and coughed. My little bed-room was within earshot of the Scott-Brownings' stables and I could hear him hacking and racking away, it was pitiful.

One November morning I crept out into the foggy darkness, with a shawl over me head and hands in mittens and whispered over the wall, and only that Ethel whispered back.

'Where's Mason then?' I says, and Ethel tells me he's been put off. 'Missus says he's slacking off the work,' she tells me. 'They're going to get a girl instead, because girls is stronger.'

'Where's he gone to?' I asks. It really upset me. Weather like what we were having, mists straight up from the river and a smack of frost to it.

'Dunno,' that Ethel says. 'He just took his bundle and went. He didn't half look bad at that.'

Three mornings later Mason was under the wall again – dear knows where he had been in the meantime for he looked terrible. Some boys had pinched his bundle, and he hadn't eaten since he'd been turned off. He was shivering and quite wore out.

'I'm lying up at the stables for a bit,' he whispers. 'It was the only place I could think of. No one will know, they never goes there.'

'Does Ethel know?' I asks. And he says, no, she's weak he says, 'She'd be bound to let on to save herself in case they found out later.'

'You go back then,' I says, 'And I'll find you something hot and I'll bring it as soon as I can.'

After me Miss had had her breakfast I drained off the tea from the pot and warmed it up in a little saucepan with some sugar and a pinch of ginger like our mam did for fevers, and when it was ready I poured it into a tin can with a lid.

It wasn't easy for me to get down that wall with the drink and all, but I managed somehow. I found the track through the trees that led to the stables and I let myself in.

It wasn't half a dark old cobwebby ruin of a place and didn't it stink! I reckon it had been left just as it was when the last horse had been led out of it.

Mason had made a bed for himself up in the loft, all among the damp and mouldy hay. I couldn't hardly see him it was so dark. I felt for his face and it was as hot as fire. He drank the tea and almost at once he dropped off to sleep and when he slept his breath was raspy like an old, old man's.

I went back to our place by the roadway, through the Scott-Browning's side-gate and managed it without me Miss finding out. Ours was quite a small place – no more than a cottage really, but when Miss Johnson was in her little parlour with her fire and her books she never heard a thing. I slipped off two more times to take a look at poor Mason. Each time he seemed worse than before. He got light-headed and didn't know me, and then he cried to himself like a baby. It was awful to hear him going on so in the smelly old dark.

There was only one thing to do, and that was to tell Miss. So I did. I owned up to everything. The scraps that didn't get to Mr Williams' bucket and all.

'In the stable, in this weather?' Miss Johnson says. 'Why didn't you tell me before, you silly, silly child? We must move him at once.'

We wrapped ourselves up and went round to the Scott-Browningses there and then. Miss tatted on the door without stop till that Ethel opened it. She said her Master and Missus were out for the day and me Miss said, perhaps it was just as well, for she might not be able to keep her hands off them. She *was* in a state.

So then we went round to the stable – me, Miss J. and that scared Ethel, who was afraid of what her Missus would say, and afraid of Miss Johnson, and not too sure of me, either.

Poor Mason was rough-bad by now and he breathed all the time like he was choking. Miss sent that snivelling Ethel back to the house for blankets and a lamp, and me down to the High Street for one of the doctors. And after he'd looked at poor Mason the doctor sent me back to the High Street again to fetch a policeman.

That Ethel just stood at the back saying, 'Oh, what will *they* say about the blankets. You'll tell them I didn't know he was here,' – over and over till me Miss got mad with her and told her to hold her tongue, she was upsetting the boy.

There was only one place for Mason then, and that was Miss Johnson's cottage in the spare bedroom where her nice lady friends stayed when they made their genteel summer visits.

I got a fire going and Ethel warmed bricks in the oven for the bed. Then the constable carried poor Mason down the loft ladder and round the road to our place and Miss and the doctor got him to bed. He was coughing and muttering and light-headed all the time.

Ethel was so frightened she wouldn't go back to the big house to face her Master, so me Miss said she could stay the night with us. You should have seen the supper she ate! Mine as well as her own, for I was too upset to eat. She kept wondering what the Scott-Brownings would think when they got back to a cold house and no supper.

Gossip spreads like butter in hot weather! Next day ladies were in and out with jars of jelly and cups of broth, with ears a-flap and cries of outrage, and from what I could judge there wasn't much to choose between their behaviour and the way people acted down our way when there had been a scandalous happening. The Vicar came with a big gentleman in checked trousers who was in a rare old state of rage. He was a newspaper writer. He and the Vicar went in afterwards to see the Scott-Browningses. I don't know what was said, or how it came out in the papers, but it must have been hot, for those fat frauds moved from the district soon afterwards.

That Ethel got another post very quick with a dear old widow-lady who made a right pet of her. In fact, she was really spoiled and uppish in the end, and could hardly even nod at me when we met at the shops. Miss Johnson said people often acted that way towards folks who'd helped them. In the end she married and left our part of the world. I was glad none of my brothers had met and married her, when I think of those squashed beetles and things. Still, in fairness, it *was* Mason who'd put her up to that.

What about Mason? Well, it was sad really, but he was poor and unwanted and he'd never had enough nourishment inside him to fight back on. No. The morning after me Miss took him in I woke up early with that Ethel snoring like a full pig beside me, and I crept across the landing to the spare bedroom, and

there he was, and there *she* was: me nice Miss. She was fast asleep and holding his hand and him quite cold and dead – the poor little cock-sparrow.

Dick he thought his first name was. Dick Mason. And that's all anyone will ever know about him.

Well, you might think that's a very sad story to end up on, as sad as any of the Prize books me sister Aggie used to read aloud of a Sunday afternoon, the ones that are all about kind ladies reading the Bible to poor ragged children who take sickly and die and go to heaven.

My Miss Johnson was very cut up at the time. She cried and cried as if poor Mason had been a near relation instead of the like of what he was. So I told her, if them books was anything to go by, I reckoned Dick would have been took up by the angels straightaway for he'd been ragged and sickly enough, dear knows.

'He'll be all right,' I tells her, 'three hot meals a day and a nice white outfit and wings to get around with and no one to hustle him about.' I went on and on laying it out to cheer her up and in the end she laughed a bit. She says, 'Let's hope it's just as you say, for I expect that was his idea of heaven. He deserves it. He never harmed anyone, poor lamb.'

Nor he did, except for giving Ethel that squashed beetle idea, and who knows they could well have been nourishing anyway for, do you know, that stuff that makes them iced cakes pink is made of red beetles? Miss Johnson told me so, and pink iced cakes are lovely. Yes, I reckon he's up there somewhere and all I hope is I won't be so bad that they shut the gate at me when my time comes.